The Legacy Paradox

Galactic Conspiracies 3

Rob Colton

The Degan Paradox:

Galactic Conspiracies 3

©2015 Rob Colton

http://www.robcolton.com

Cover art by Slumberus – http://slumberus.deviantart.com

The Degan Paradox
Galactic Conspiracies 3

The adventure continues in this action-packed follow up to The Degan Incident *and* The Cassini Mission*!*

Peri McSmith is aboard the U.S.C. *Cassini*, en route to the Degan Homeworld. A routine medical examination reveals a startling yet impossible link between Peri and the *Cassini*'s last mission.

Beshel Drago, Chief Investigator for the Degan Federation, searches for leads on the rogue scientists conducting illegal genetic experiments using Degan citizens. He hits yet another a dead end—until the rescued embryo's human parent is identified.

When the Degan Science Institute is attacked, and the embryo stolen, it's up to Beshel and Peri to not only recover the child, but to prevent all-out war between the Degans and the Galactic Planetary Union.

Special Thanks

Thank you to all the Degan fans who have been asking for Peri's story from the beginning.

Chapter 1

Perin McSmith picked up the last item on top of his dresser. Instead of immediately packing it away in his box, Peri stopped and took a good look at it. He couldn't help the smile that spread across his face. It was a picture of him and his best friend, Devin. Taken when they were younger, it was one of his favorites.

He remembered the day like it was yesterday. It was the night before his high school graduation. They'd gone out to celebrate one last time before school was out, just him and Dev.

That next week Peri would start his brand new job at Spaceport Prime, the largest port on the North American continent servicing flights bound for space travel. Dev had been working as a docking gate technician for the past year and was able to get Peri an interview. Dev put in a good word with the supervisor, and Peri got the job.

It was a time of big changes for Peri. Not only was he leaving school and the orphanage he'd lived in all his life, but he was starting a new career and moving into a new apartment.

All he had to do was find a man and life would be complete.

Of course, things didn't always work out the way you planned them.

Peri was grateful for his friend. Devin was always there for him. Growing up in the McSmith Group Home for Boys, they'd bonded almost from the start. They were more than just friends; they were brothers. Not that anyone would mistake them as blood related. Peri was thinner, and had wavy black hair and brown eyes. He'd always wished he had Devin's pretty blond hair.

He placed the picture into the box and sealed it. That was the last of it. Anything not included with the pre-furnished apartment had already been sold. Where Peri was going, he would only need his clothes and personal belongings.

Never in a million years did he think he'd be packing up and moving across the galaxy. Dev was the one who yearned to travel the stars and see what was beyond the solar system. Peri had no such desires. It never occurred to him that he might actually leave the planet.

But seeing how happy Devin was in his new home, he was a little envious. He found himself missing his friend something fierce. Sure they video chatted regularly and Devin sent pictures, but it wasn't the same.

The planet Dega was so beautiful. It was no wonder Devin wanted to stay.

It was the perfect place to raise a family. That's what Devin was doing. He was living with Bastian Drago, his bondmate. They had a son, Callan, who was the cutest little thing Peri had ever seen. Half-human and half-Degan, he took the best traits from each of his dads and made a perfect little baby. And now Devin was pregnant again.

Peri really had a hard time wrapping his brain around the whole situation. First Bastian bonded with Devin. Peri didn't really understand the specifics, but Dev said it was like they were soulmates. What really freaked him out was the pregnancy thing. Something about Bastian's DNA changed Devin's body so he could make a baby... a once-in-a-lifetime freak mutation. It was just so wrong. But damn, they sure made a cute baby.

It took Peri some time to get up the courage to make the move, but he did it. He was leaving Earth and moving to Dega.

Okay, so getting fired from his job at the spaceport was a big help in pushing him to make the change. He'd been late one too many times, according to his supervisor. Besides, it was only a matter of time before his job was replaced by the new automated docking operating system.

Whatever.

* * * *

Going to the spaceport as a passenger instead of an employee was... strange. Peri had actually never travelled via the spaceport before.

He had plenty of time to get to his gate, so Peri leisurely strolled along the walkway, lugging a rolling trunk and a small suitcase with him. Luckily, Dev had arranged for the rest of his boxes to be picked up and taken straight to the ship to be delivered on arrival. Not that he had all that much stuff, but he was glad he didn't have to worry about it.

Passengers of all species moved around him, some fast, some slow. He passed one of the gates that was closed down for renovation. Noisy construction workers and technicians installed the upgrades that would've put Peri out of work.

Pulling out his comPad, he double-checked his departure gate. He was catching a shuttle from gate Alpha-04. The shuttle would take him to Luna Station. The station orbited the moon, and that was where the ship that would actually take him to the planet Dega was docked.

His ex-supervisor, Roble, manned the gate. Even though the guy had fired him, Peri didn't harbor any bad feelings toward the man.

Peri gave the man a genuine smile, and placed his hand on the scanner. The computer chirped a pleasant tone, and the scanner flashed green as it announced, *Perin McSmith, cleared for boarding.*

Roble gave Peri a crooked smile as he held out his hand. "Goodbye, Peri, and good luck."

"Thank you." Peri shook his hand, then turned toward the spaceway. With a deep breath, he walked to the shuttle that would take him away from the planet that had been his home.

Peri's heart nearly leapt out of his chest when the shuttle took off, but it was quickly slammed back inside. It felt as if he had a lead weight on him. Gripping the armrests as tight as he could, he squeezed his eyes shut and prayed to whoever would listen he would make it out alive.

The shuttle shook so hard, he thought it was going to fly apart. The pressure in his chest hurt, making it difficult to breathe. He just knew gravity was going to pull the ship back down to Earth. It was certainly trying to pull his stomach back, and Peri didn't want to think about where it would come out.

Suddenly everything stopped. The pressure was gone and the shaking became a subtle vibration.

Opening his eyes, Peri looked out the window as the ship emerged from Earth's atmosphere. Blue faded away to black. Twinkling stars filled his view.

"Wow," he whispered to himself.

Maybe Dev had the right idea.

* * * *

Peri's mouth fell open as soon as he stepped onto the station. In sharp contrast to the aging Spaceport Prime, everything on Luna Station felt new and clean. The surfaces shined brightly, as if they'd just been polished. Everything was well lit. Abundant digital signage displayed in multiple languages—including some alien—made it easy to find where you needed to go next.

Though he had plenty of time to grab a bite to eat, Peri decided to forego lunch. After that shuttle launch, he wasn't sure he'd be able to keep anything down. Maybe he could get settled on his transport ship a little early.

He stopped at one of the docking terminal kiosks and set down his trunk and suitcase. Maybe he should have checked the trunk with his other belongings. He was getting tired of dragging it around.

Peri tapped the screen. "Uh, computer, where is my departure gate?"

The computer screen indicated it required Peri's identification. Peri placed his hand on the screen inside the outline of the hand.

After a moment, the computer displayed a map and announced, *U.S.C. Cassini docked at platform 12A. Departing for the Alpha Ursae Majoris system at 1400 hours.*

Peri looked around to get his bearings, then began the walk to the docking gate.

The transparent glass overhead gave him a breathtaking view of the ship. Not just a ship, but a Navy cruiser. It looked brand new, not even a single scratch marred its perfectly smooth hull.

This was the vessel taking him to his destination? There had to be a mistake. He double-checked the sign over the spaceway's airlock. Platform 12A.

Spotting a pair of Navy security officers manning the gate, Peri walked over to the human men. "Excuse me. Is this the *Cassini*, heading to the Degan homeworld?"

"Yes, sir."

"What kind of ship is this?"

"The U.S.C. *Cassini* Mark-II is a *Zeta*-class Union Navy scout cruiser," the officer proudly boasted. "Newly commissioned, top of the line. Are you ready to board, sir?"

How cool was it that he was getting to hitch a ride on a top-of-the-line Navy cruiser? Devin apparently had a lot of pull. Peri knew Dev's mother-in-law worked closely with the Degan Prime Minister and they'd arranged for free transport, but he hadn't expected this. He figured he'd be making the trip on a garbage scowl or something, not traveling in luxury on one of the Navy's new flagships.

Trying to play it cool, he replied with a shrug, "Yes, I'm ready."

Peri placed his hand on the scanner, and the computer beeped. *Perin McSmith, cleared for boarding.*

"Thank you." He gave the security man a smile and made his way down the spaceway.

A gigantic hunk of Marine standing at ease greeted him at the airlock. Built like a prime stud, he was totally hot in a rugged, throw-you-over-his-shoulder-and-drag-you-to-his-cave kind of way. He certainly filled out his uniform well. Peri let his eyes drift from the marine's chest to his groin. *Very well.* Peri had never seen a human man so large. So very large in all the right places. Unfortunately, he was wearing a wedding band on his left ring finger.

Damn. Why were all the good ones taken?

"Good morning, Mr. McSmith. I am Sergeant Kane Robertson, chief security and tactical officer. I'll be showing you to your assigned quarters."

The Marine seemed very formal and wound up tighter than a monkey's nuts. Peri figured he might as well have a little fun. "Hello.

You can call me Peri. Can you get my things, please?"

Sergeant Robertson blinked. "Excuse me?"

Peri pointed to his belongings. "That chest and suitcase. Thank you."

Robertson ground his teeth together, and then plastered on the fakest smile Peri had ever seen. "I'll have them brought to your room. This way…"

The security chief escorted Peri down the hall, to a turbolift. As they approached, the doors opened automatically and the lift's internal lights activated.

"Sweet. Say, I'm a little hungry. Can I order room service, or is there a restaurant on board?"

"The mess hall is on Deck 2. You can help yourself to whatever has been prepared."

"Oh. So, what is there to do for fun?"

The muscle in the man's jaw twitched. "This isn't a cruise ship."

Peri tried hard to suppress his smile, but wasn't certain how successful he was. "Oh. You know, I've never been on a starship before. What if I get motion sickness?"

"The *Cassini* has state of the art motion stabilizers, but Sickbay is also on Deck 2. If you'll excuse me…"

After showing him to the room, the Marine couldn't get away fast enough.

The assigned quarters weren't very big, but the room itself was quite nice. Everything looked brand new. It even smelled brand new, like when they installed new carpet at the spaceport. The outer wall consisted of one large window showing off a lovely view of Luna Station.

He ran a hand over the bed, liking the way the fluffy comforter felt against his fingertips. Maybe he would get a nice nap in.

The room had its own little bathroom, complete with a sonic shower. Peri had never used one before, and he was looking forward to trying it out.

After using the bathroom, he washed his hands and returned to the main cabin. He looked out the window just in time to see the ship pulling away from the station.

Unlike the shuttle departure, he hadn't even felt the ship move. Must be those state-of-the-art motion stabilizers. Maybe this trip wouldn't be so bad after all.

* * * *

"Sir?"

Degan Federation Chief Investigator Beshel Drago looked up from his comPad toward the agent who'd just entered. It was just as well. He'd read the damn intelligence report three times now and still didn't understand a word. His B Team was investigating a xenophobic faction whose protests of the influx of off-worlders were turning violent.

What the hell?

Why was he having so much trouble focusing lately? He rubbed the knot on the back of his neck, digging fingernails into his fur, in a vain attempt to ease the tension. "What is it, agent?"

He hadn't meant to snap at Agent Barlan, and he tried to ease his tone with a facsimile of a smile.

Beshel's second-in-command was fair-furred, though he had a noticeable scar bisecting the fur near his left cranial horn. Likely a battle injury. Not unlike Beshel, he was a bit on the shorter side for an adult Degan male, but made up for it in the width of his shoulders and generous muscle mass.

Barlan raised a brow. "If I may be blunt… you look like shit. Sir."

"It's this damn rock. The sooner we get off it…" Beshel set his comPad on the desk, turning it slightly so it was lined up perfectly parallel to the sheet of paper already there.

"Agreed, sir. I'm ready to get home."

Beshel turned and glanced out the window. Chunks of metal and concrete littered the landscape of ruined, crumbling buildings. The road into the facility was riddled with muddy potholes large enough to swallow a Degan battleship.

He longed to return to the lush vegetation that covered his homeworld.

Centauri Colony was a shithole, to be frank. The human colony had been decimated years ago during their war with the Mirans, back before Earth joined the Galactic Planetary Union. Today, most of the planet was still abandoned, left in ruins. Not that it was a gem before the war. The world was little more than a barren ball of mud, stripped completely bare of any natural resources that might have been even remotely valuable.

Only two kinds of people made Centauri Colony their home these days: those with questionable mental capacity who were attempting to live off the grid because the universe was out to get them... or those with something to hide.

After the destruction of the illegal research colony on XP-8460 by the U.S.C. *Cassini*, Beshel's investigation traced the lab manifests here. His team was currently working with a Union task force to clean up any illegal experiments. Though the Degan Federation and the Union had their differences, one thing they agreed on was the outlawing of genetic experimentation that did not relate to infectious disease eradication. Certainly not for military purposes. It seems some humans had forgotten this. The things they did splicing human and Degan DNA were horrific.

Relations between the Degan Federation and the Galactic Planetary Union were already rocky. This scandal only brought further tension between the two governments. The fact they were cooperating with the Degans in the clean-up didn't do much to ease the tension. That wasn't anything against Corporal Durant, or his men. The Marines had been picked especially for this mission by the Union commission investigating the incident on XP-8460. They were working side-by-side with Beshel's team, and Beshel found them to be upstanding and trustworthy.

As Beshel stared out toward the horizon, it started to rain. Again. With the rain, a drop in temperature would come. The last thing

Beshel wanted to be was cold and wet. No Degan in the history of *ever* wanted to be cold and wet.

I hate this damn place.

Beshel turned back toward his second. "Did you grow up on the homeworld, Barlan?"

"No, sir. Dubhe Colony," he replied proudly. "First Colony."

"Ah. Lovely planet. Though I can't abide your winters."

Dubhe was the closest inhabitable planetary system to the Degan Homeworld, orbiting Alpha Ursae Majoris's smaller companion star. Shortly after their species gained interstellar travel, the world was colonized, and the two binary stars gave birth to the Degan Federation. That was many centuries ago. The Degan Federation now encompassed six major star systems, plus many minor colonies within its borders. It was home to billions of citizens, mostly Degan, though there was a growing population of off-worlders living within their borders.

"Nothing like the cold air to get your blood flowing. It might do you some good."

Beshel doubted it. He wanted to bask in the warm sun, not bundle up in a parka. Though it did explain the lighter coloring of Barlan's fur. Many descendants of so-called First Colony were fairer furred. "Yes. Right. What have you got?"

"Working with the Union Marines, we have completed an inventory of the lab."

"Good. Have all biological components been destroyed?"

"Corporal Durant's men are working on it now."

"Make sure at least one of our team members is present at all times. Not that I don't trust the Union men, but this happened on their watch."

"Yes, sir." Barlan nodded curtly, turned on his heel, and left the office.

With a sigh, Beshel picked up his comPad and began to read— again.

Chapter 2

"Peri."

Hearing his name growled like that sent a shiver down his spine. No one had ever wanted him like this. And he knew no one else ever would.

He reached up and pulled the big alien's body down. Peri was well aware the Degan was much taller than him, but when he was flat on his back and the alien atop of him, his massive, wide torso covered him fully. Hard, fur-covered muscles pinned him down on the carpet.

Peri's hands roamed, scraping his nails across the expansive back, completely covered in soft, honey-colored fur. Who would have thought all that body hair would be so damn sexy?

A moan fell from his lips. He spread his legs wider to accommodate the Degan's body. "Please...."

They were on the floor, half-eaten Chinese take-out boxes scattered around them. Normally, Peri would have been appalled, but right now he didn't care. Reaching a hand between their bodies, he found the hard cock that jutted from between the alien's legs. He'd known from talking to Devin that Degan males were well-endowed, but the flesh in his hands felt *enormous*—scalding hot, already slick with secreted juices.

With a growl, the man began to move above him. He thrust into Peri's fist, the copious pre-cum lubricating the way.

He sniffed a trail up Peri's neck. "So good." His tongue along followed along the same path.

Peri couldn't help but bare his neck, letting him have whatever he wanted.

The Degan's mouth covered his in a brutal kiss. His tongue plundered Peri's mouth as his hips picked up speed, thrusting into

Peri's fist. His slippery erection rubbed against Peri's body, making Peri delirious with need. He moaned around Besh's tongue, arching his body up, needing the contact.

That cock was huge, but he would take it. He wanted it inside so damn bad. He would give it to him, anything he wanted.

Next time.

This time he was too close. He was going to come. Bringing his other hand between their bodies, Peri grabbed Besh's shaft with both hands, using a double-fisting action to bring his partner off. He twisted, milking him, making him crazy, judging from the grunts and growls.

The Degan threw his head back and let out a loud groan. Liquid heat erupted like a geyser from the end of his cock, pulsing in jets over and over, coating Peri's body from the hollow of his neck to the wisps of hair surrounding his groin.

"Besh!"

Peri jerked hard, nearly falling out of bed.

Bolting upright, he drew in a series of gasping breaths. He was drenched with sweat. Sticky fluid covered his belly, caught in the hairs surrounding the base of his still-throbbing dick.

Like all the other times, the dream felt real.

It wasn't the first time he'd woken up like this. He didn't understand why he was dreaming about Beshel Drago like this. He didn't even like that stupid Degan, and Besh sure as heck didn't like him. They never had sex.

Peri would have remembered that.

He fell back onto the pillow and immediately regretted it when his head was slapped with a cold wetness. He lifted up and threw the sopping sweat-soaked pillow onto the floor. He rolled over to the other side of the bed where it was dry.

But now he was wide-awake. He craned his head back, looking toward the window. Stars streaked past at a dizzying speed, and Peri had to squeeze his eyes shut when the room began to spin.

Maybe he was imagining things, but he started to feel sick to his stomach. It had to be from the ship's motion.

State of the art stabilizers, my ass.

Peri slid out of bed and went to the bathroom to try out the sonic shower.

* * * *

After stopping to ask a crewman for directions, he finally found the sickbay on Deck 2, near the center of the ship.

Although there were no patients, the ward bustled with activity.

The head of each empty, high-tech bed was surrounded by computer displays. A pair of doctors moved between them, tapping at the controls, running some type of diagnostic. Nurses inventoried supply cabinets. A doctor in a lab coat stood in the back corner at a workstation, fiddling with some cylindrical contraption that was connected to the computer display.

"Can I help you?"

The woman's voice startled Peri. He turned to find an attractive woman smiling. Like the man in the back, she wore a white lab coat over her standard Navy-issued uniform.

"Hi. I think I'm feeling motion sickness."

"Hmm. Most people don't feel the effects of the motion dampeners, but a very small number of people *are* sensitive. Why don't we check you out?"

He followed her to one of the beds and hopped up to sit on the end.

"I'm Dr. Moore."

"I'm Peri McSmith." He shook the doctor's hand.

"Ah, yes. Our VIP passenger. It's a pleasure to meet you, Peri."

"That's me," he said with a grin. "VIP."

Dr. Moore chuckled politely.

Peri lay back on the table and let the doctor perform her scan. With a comPad in one hand, she waved a wand across his body. After the scan was complete, she took a swab of the inside of his cheek. She placed it into the computer's scanning drawer.

"It'll just take a few minutes to run the tests," she said. "I don't see any physical signs of imbalance, but I can give you a mild anti-emetic to treat your symptoms."

A what now? "Okay…"

Dr. Moore returned a few moments later with a hypospray injector. She pressed it to Peri's arm. A hiss and a quick sting, and it was over.

"That should do it," she said. "If your symptoms worsen, please see me right away."

"I will, Doctor. Thank you."

Peri sat up, then hopped off the bed.

A series of rapid beeps came from the back corner, sounding urgent enough to draw both of their attention.

The man at the back workstation tapped away at his computer for a moment, then looked up and met Peri's eyes. His intense gaze never left as he called out, "Dr. Moore. I need to talk to you about the DNA sample you just catalogued into the Union database.…"

Chapter 3

Beshel slammed the door control as soon as he entered the facility. "God damn this place," he muttered as he shook his head, trying to get rid of some of the water that had soaked into his fur.

It was fucking raining again. It was cold. And it was a dead end. The combination set Beshel's mood straight to hell.

"Chief Drago?"

Beshel slowed to let the Union Marine officer catch up to him. "Corporal Durant?"

Durant was human, but one of the biggest Beshel had seen. He was clearly one of Earth's genetically enhanced military units, GEMs they called them. When Earth joined the Union, the practice had been abolished, and the men were absorbed into the Union armed forces with the rest of Earth's military. They also passed their enhancements down to their children. Durant was likely second generation.

"Union HQ has recalled us. We're to return to Sargan III." The over-sized human handed Beshel a comPad with the digitally signed orders.

Beshel read it over. Durant and his unit were being transferred to the U.S.C. *Artemis*. He returned the pad to the man. "Thank you."

"Do you have any further leads, sir? If so, I could convince my commanding officer to extend our assignment. I really want to catch these fuckers."

Beshel shook his head and bit back a growl. "I wish I had better news. Our intelligence agents have hit a dead end. I've gone over all of the reports myself so many times I can recite them from memory." Beshel reached back and kneaded the knot on his neck. "Unfortunately, with no new reports… But, trust me, we won't stop looking."

"Very good, Chief. It's been a pleasure working with you. If there's anything I can do to help, let me know."

"Likewise, Corporal."

* * * *

"Just a moment, Peri."

Dr. Moore closed the door behind her, leaving him alone in her private office.

The way she and the other doctor were whispering to each other made him nervous. He knew damn well they were talking about him because they kept glancing his way. And then the guy wanted to see his internal scans.

Oh, god, what if I'm dying?

Peri used his hand to fan himself. *Was it getting hot in here?*

Trying to keep himself occupied, Peri looked around the office. Besides the desk and chairs, the room was empty. There weren't even any pictures on the walls. Shouldn't she have diplomas or certificates hanging up? Not that Peri thought she was some kind of quack...

Boxes were piled up along one wall. So the doctor hadn't unpacked her things yet. Maybe her credentials were in there. One box on top was unsealed. He leaned forward, and used a finger to lift a flap, then scoped out the contents.

The door opened, and Peri jerked away from the boxes. The doctor entered, followed by the man.

Dr. Moore took the chair behind her desk. She had an uneasy smile on her face.

"Hi, Peri." The male doctor held out his hand. "I'm Dr. Aron Adler."

Though hesitant, Peri still shook his hand to be polite. "Hello, Doctor..."

"You can call me Aron. I'm the ship's lead science officer. Why don't you have a seat?"

Aron sat down in one of the chairs, and Peri sat next to him. Only then did Peri notice the scientist's uniform accent colors were different than the doctor's—blue instead of green. It must be really bad if he needed a doctor *and* the lead scientist. Gripping the chair's arm rests, he braced himself for the bad news.

"As you know, we're heading to Alpha Ursae Majoris IV, the Degan homeworld."

"Yes, I know. That's why I'm hitching a ride." He glanced between the scientist and the doctor.

"The nature of our mission is classified, but I've been given permission to discuss certain aspects with you."

"Me? Why? Is this about my friend Devin?"

"No." Aron exchanged a glance with Dr. Moore. "I know this is a delicate question, and I wouldn't ask it normally..."

"Oh my god, will someone please tell me what's going on? You are both freaking me out."

"Okay, Peri." Aron drew in a deep breath and let it out slowly. "Do you know any Degans?"

"Of course. I've met Devin's husband, Bastian. I also know Bastian's uncle, Beshel. There were a couple others who worked for Besh who I met once."

"That's not quite what I meant. How can I put this...? Have you had sex with a Degan?"

Peri's mouth dropped open in horror. "What? No!"

"Are you sure?"

"I think I would know if I ever had a hairy, seven-foot beast on top of me."

"Aron," Dr. Moore interrupted. "I told you, the internal scans were normal."

"But he matches the DNA profile ninety-nine-point-nine-nine-nine percent."

"What are you talking about?"

"The reason we are en route to the Degan homeworld is to return an embryo. At this time, it is suspended in cryogenic sleep."

"What does that have to do with me?"

"It's... Well... It's yours."

"Mine?"

"You are one of its fathers. An unknown Degan is the other."

* * * *

After throwing up into the commode, the two doctors helped Peri to one of the medical beds. The room swirled and pitched as Peri's knees gave way. He vaguely felt the pinch of a hyospray on his neck. Within minutes, his stomach calmed itself, and his vertigo passed.

Dr. Moore patted his shoulder before walking off to take care of the empty hyospray.

"I know it's a shock, Peri..." Aron let his voice trail off.

"You said 'fathers.' So the DNA matches me and a *male* Degan?"

"Yes. That's correct."

"How? Wait, it's not Bastian's DNA is it? Devin's husband?" *Oh god, that would be too weird.*

"No, it doesn't belong to Bastian. As for the how... well, that's the million-dollar question, isn't it? According to your internal scans, you don't have a womb, like your friend Devin. It would appear the embryo was grown *outside* your body. If it's all right with you, I'd like to use your DNA to run some tests."

Remembering what Devin had gone through, Peri was wary of scientists running tests. He looked at Aron suspiciously. "I don't know..."

"I assure you, it would be completely non-invasive. It would only be computer simulations based on both of your DNA profiles."

"Can I see it?"

"There's not much to see, but of course you can."

Aron helped Peri up, then led him to the back corner. Sitting on the workstation table, a cylindrical object was connected to the computer with a series of cables. Inside was a pink fluid, and floating in the middle was... *it*. To be honest, Peri wasn't sure what it was exactly. It was about the size of a golf ball and didn't really look like a baby.

"The portable cryo-chamber is keeping it safe until we arrive on Dega."

Aron pulled up a chair, and Peri sat down to get a better look at the little bundle of cells.

"What happens when it reaches Dega?"

"It'll be handed over to the Degan Science Institute."

"Oh..."

"I'll be over there if you need me."

Peri nodded his head, acknowledging Aron's words, but he wasn't really paying attention to him. He couldn't take his eyes off the contents of the cylinder. Leaning in close, he placed a hand on the container's glass wall.

What Aron told him was impossible. But still... He didn't know how he knew, but deep in his soul, he knew it was true. This was going to grow into a baby. *His* baby.

And despite the bizarre situation, Peri found himself grinning.

"It looks like I'm your daddy, little fella."

* * * *

It took three days for the *Cassini* to arrive at the Degan homeworld. During that time, Peri spent most of it in sickbay, sitting with the "embryo" as Aron called it.

Aron stood behind Peri, and peered at the embryo over his shoulder. "The embryo will be taken to the Science Institute in the Capital City. The Degan scientists want to unfreeze it, then transfer it to an incubation chamber."

"Will that hurt it?"

"No. It will grow normally at that point. The cryo-freezing process has halted its growth."

"So, it'll grow up to be a normal baby?"

"A half-human, half-Degan baby, but yes. You have no idea who the sire might be?"

Peri didn't know what to say.

Aron had asked more than once if he knew who the *sire* might be. Of course, he had a good guess, but he didn't tell him that. It would be too weird to explain.

"I don't know."

Okay, so he had *dreams* about Besh. But they had *never* had *sex*. Peri would remember if they did. And now that he thought about it, even in the dreams they didn't have actual sex. It was only kissing and touching, no penetration. Each time, it started out innocent enough. He'd stop by to help pack up Devin's personal belongings. They ordered Chinese take-out. A chopstick demonstration somehow turned into a make-out session.

"Have you decided what you want to do?"

"Do?"

"With the baby. Once the incubator cycle finishes, it will need to be cared for." Aron placed a hand on Peri's shoulder. "If you would like to give him up for adoption, no one will judge you. The Degans will make sure he finds a happy home."

Peri shook his head violently. "No!" He blew out a breath and calmed his voice. "I mean, I want him."

How could he give him up? He would *never* subject his child to that. The way he grew up in that group home, getting passed over time and time again. No one wanted him. There was always someone better... someone younger, cuter, smarter... No. No way would Peri put this baby through that. He would come home with Peri, and he would be taken care of. He would be *loved*.

"Peri?"

Peri jumped at the sound of Aron's voice. He turned away from his offspring and looked back at Aron. "Sorry?"

Aron had been joined by the Marine who greeted him when he first arrived. The two were standing very close. Only then did Peri realize that Aron was married to Sergeant Robertson.

"We're approaching Degan station," Robertson said. "I'm sorry, but you need to head back to your quarters while we dock."

"Do I have to?" he asked, looking between Robertson and Aron.

"I'm afraid so," Aron said. "All non-ship personnel must be secured in quarters during docking."

"You'll take care of him, right?"

"Of course. I'll let you know right away once he's set up at the Science Institute. You can come visit him then."

"Okay. Thank you, Aron, for everything."

"Of course, Peri."

Peri gave the portable cryo-chamber one last look before leaving sickbay.

Chapter 4

When the *Cassini* finally arrived at Degan Space Station Gamma and docked, Peri was greeted by an obscenely pregnant Devin and his family.

Devin wore a cream-colored linen tunic and a chocolate brown leather kilt. The front of his shirt bulged out as if he was smuggling a basketball underneath.

Bastian stood by his side, looking like a giant, wearing the same style kilt but with a matching leather vest. He held the hand of a half-human/half-Degan toddler, their son Callan, who was dressed like Devin. His bushy mop of honey blond hair was long enough it began to curl at the ends. With chubby pink cheeks, and a pair of little horns on top of his head, he looked cute enough to eat with a spoon.

"Per!" Devin called out, standing on his tiptoes, waving his hand over his head like mad, as if a pregnant human male didn't stick out amongst all of the Degans and other aliens.

Letting go of his trunk and suitcase, Peri ran to his best friend, threw his arms around him, and held on tight. He tried to ignore the way Devin's distended stomach was pushing against him.

"I missed you so much," he whispered.

"I missed you, too."

"Nice skirt, by the way."

Devin laughed, and shook his hips, making the kilt flap. "Why, thank you, kind sir."

With everything that was going on, Peri knew he would need to rely on Dev more than ever. But at the same time, he didn't know how to tell him about the baby. What could he say? *Those crazy scientists who tortured you somehow stole my DNA. And bippity-boppity-boo, here's a baby.*

Over Devin's shoulder, Peri watched Aron pushing a cart containing the embryo's portable cryo-freezer. He was joined by a unit of Degans in military uniforms, as well as a pair that looked like scientists. Aron looked over his shoulder and gave Peri a sympathetic smile with a thumbs up sign.

"Everything okay?" Devin asked.

Turning his attention back to Devin, Peri nodded. "Yes. I'm great." He separated from Devin and looked down at his belly. "You look like you're going to pop."

"Lord knows I feel like it." Devin rubbed his hand over his belly. "Come meet Callan."

Bastian reached out and rubbed a hand down Peri's back, giving him an awkward sideways hug. "It is good to see you, Peri."

"Thank you, Bastian. You too." He squatted down in front of Callan. "Well, look at you, cutie pie. You're so big! How did you get so big? Give your Uncle Peri a hug."

"'Kay," he said in a small, squeaky voice.

Callan leaned in and wrapped his arms around Peri's neck and squeezed.

Peri was suddenly overwhelmed with emotion. "Oh." He closed his eyes and held his innocent little nephew, imagining one day soon he would have one just like him. Someone who would love him unconditionally.

Once they reached the hover car, Bastian took Peri's luggage and effortlessly tossed them into the storage area, all while holding tightly to Callan's hand. It was a good thing. The boy was curious about everything, and tugged at his sire's hand, trying to run off.

"How old is Callan?" Peri asked.

"He's almost a year."

"God, he's so big."

"Yeah, he definitely takes after his dad."

"And you got another one on the way so soon. You're crazy."

"Well, we didn't plan on having another one, but the birth

control kinda didn't work."

"Obviously. Do you know what you're having yet?" he asked, looking down at Devin's belly.

"We're having a girl this time. Here." Dev took Peri's hand and placed it on his stomach.

Peri resisted the urge to rudely jerk his hand away. "I'm sorry, but that is just freaky."

Devin laughed softly. "You get used to it."

"I'll have to take your word for—" A flutter of movement under Peri's hand surprised him. "Oh!"

"I know."

Peri looked at Dev wide-eyed. "Oh, there it is again." His apprehension turned to curiosity, which turned to awe. "Wow…"

"She's not as feisty as her big brother was, but she does her share of moving around."

"Yeah, well, it feels like she's ready to come out."

Devin laughed. "Maybe. But *we're* not ready."

Peri couldn't help but smile as he watched Devin walk. He had this cute little waddle, and Peri was tempted to tease him about it, but not while over-protective Bastian was hovering.

* * * *

Yet another shuttle. This one would take them from Degan Station down to the surface. Thankfully, this one was nice and smooth. There was not even a hint of turbulence as they entered the planet Dega's atmosphere.

Once they arrived planet-side, they made their way to the parking deck where Bastian's hovercar was located.

"Fancy," Peri noted. The hovercar was jet black, sleek and shiny. He'd never been in one before, and despite being carted from one ship to another, he was actually looking forward to the ride.

Bastian opened the car door and got Callan situated into his seat. He hurried around Peri, took Devin by the arm and guided him gently into the car's passenger seat.

Devin looked over at Peri and rolled his eyes as his husband buckled his shoulder strap, giving it a tug to make sure Devin was secure. "Bastian thinks I'm going to break."

A flash of pain crossed Bastian's face. "You almost did, my true one."

Reaching up, Devin stroked Bastian's furry jaw. "Not with you around to take care of me."

Swallowing, Peri turned away from their intimate display.

The car ride was simply amazing. Peri had never seen anything like it. Though the vehicle whizzed along the road at high speed, there was no vibration or sense of motion at all. The ride was smooth as a baby's bottom, like riding a cloud.

Since the ride was so nice, Peri was able to concentrate on the view.

Though Devin had sent photos of the planet, they did not do the actual landscape justice. Who would have thought there could be so much grass, and so many trees? Lakes and rivers even, all of it streaking past as the car sped down the road. He was definitely not back on Earth.

Callan enjoyed the ride as much as Peri. He stared out the window the entire time. When a herd of brown furry animals came into view, he squeaked with delight and slapped his palm on the glass. To Peri, they resembled a kind of alien bison or buffalo.

"Those are saki," Devin said. "Can you say 'saki'?"

"Sahk," Callan repeated. Kind of. "Sahk, sahk, sahk…"

Peri couldn't help but smile at Devin. He was such a good dad, and Callan seemed like a good boy.

"We live a ways outside the capital, but it's worth it. You'll see."

Peri was eager to catch up with Devin, but within minutes the ride had lulled Devin to sleep.

With a smile on face, Bastian said softly, "Long rides make him sleepy, especially when he's pregnant." Bastian reached over and placed his palm on the bulge of Devin's stomach. Devin shifted slightly, but didn't wake.

Peri turned his attention back to the landscape.

By the time they arrived at Devin and Bastian's home an hour and a half later, Peri was utterly exhausted. He hadn't been sleeping well. He'd spent a lot of time in sickbay, and when he had tried to sleep, he lay in bed awake, worrying.

The sun was setting, but Peri still got a good look at the impressive home.

Situated inside an iron gate and surrounded by a forest of gigantic trees, the house was made of natural stone bricks. It sat on what seemed like an endless plot of grassy land with a small lake beyond the backyard. On the other side of the lake, there were lights from two other homes, but there were no other houses in sight.

"Watch out for our banti," Bastian said as he opened the front door.

"Your what?" Peri asked.

"Mees!" Callan squealed.

They were inside the house no more than a second when a small brown animal jumped out from nowhere. It looked like a fluffy grizzly bear cub, with a snout like a boar, and two tusks that protruded from his lower jaw. Growling and yapping, it moved in front of Peri, pushing him away from Devin and Callan.

"Mishu!" Devin snapped. "No."

The protective animal made Peri back up another step.

Bastian snapped his fingers. "Mishu. Heel."

At Bastian's command, Mishu sat down on his butt. The ball of fur glared at Peri with narrowed eyes, then stuck his tongue out.

Peri's mouth fell open. He looked over at Devin. "Did he just—"

Devin laughed. "Yeah, I know. They're too dang smart." He

looked down at the animal. "Mishu, this is Peri. He'll be staying with us. He's family." Devin moved around the banti and gave Peri a hug. "See?"

Mishu slowly approached Peri and sniffed at his leg. He let out a huff of air, then turned his attention to Callan, who got a completely opposite greeting. The little animal jumped up and down, his little legs giving him enough bounce to reach Callan's head, where he attempted to lick the boy's face. The little boy giggled up a storm while clapping his hands. Dropping down to the floor, he grabbed the furball and hugged him tight to his chest. "Mees!"

Devin watched the two best friends bond with a smile on his face. "He's a little overprotective."

Peri nodded. "Well, I can't blame him, after everything that happened."

"Let me give you a quick tour."

The house was beautifully decorated inside. Peri loved the oversized windows. The view of nature was breathtaking.

Peri covered his mouth with his hand and tried to fight back a yawn. As beautiful as their home was, and as much as he wanted to catch up with Devin, he was desperate to get some rest.

Devin smiled. "Come on. I'll show you to your room. You can take a nap. And I have *got* to pee."

* * * *

Beshel opened the front door to his home. He hit the light switch, then dropped his bag by the door. Though he was in the right place, it seemed foreign to him. It had probably been six months since he was last home. And even then, he'd only been home for a couple weeks before going back on yet another off-world assignment.

When he first took the job at the bureau, he loved traveling. Going off-world was an adventure. Sometimes he wondered if maybe this was a job best left to the younger generation. The reminder of what he did kept the citizens of the Degan Federation safe from outside threats was enough to push those thoughts away.

The air inside his home was stale and musty, and the temperature was warmer than Beshel usually liked. Using the control pad next to the front door, he activated his pre-programmed environmental settings and enabled the outside air recycling.

After kicking off his boots, he walked through the house, checking that everything looked just the way he had left it. Having only a single story, it didn't take long. It was a much bigger space than a single person needed, but he liked his home. He also liked the isolation, having no close neighbors and being near a lake.

He'd thought about getting a pet banti on more than one occasion, something that would fill up some space, and break up the quiet. Unfortunately, it seemed like his job kept him away from home more often than not. It wouldn't be fair to do that to a pet.

Beshel opened his fridge. With the exception of some out-of-date condiments, all he had was a few containers of ale. He popped one open and poured it into a mug.

Opening the sliding doors, he walked out onto his back patio. He sat down on a lounge chair and kicked back. While sipping his ale, he looked out over the lake. In the distance, he could see the lights from Bastian's house on the opposite shore.

Beshel closed his eyes. Breathing in deeply, he held the warm, clean air in his lungs before exhaling.

It was good to be home.

Chapter 5

Peri's eyes peeked opened as he woke.

It took a moment to realize where he was.

Immediately he knew he wasn't home, because his bed was nowhere near this soft and luxurious.

He couldn't remember the last time he had such a good night's sleep. The light from the orange sun peeked in through the window curtains. Pushing out of the warm comfort of the bed, Peri walked over to the window and slid the curtains back. The sky had a slight purple tint, which was odd, but otherwise everything seemed normal. Better than normal. From his window, he could see the forest and the lake.

The view from his old place was directly into the apartment building next door. And the wrinkled old guy who liked to walk around naked.

In the distance, Peri heard Devin and Callan. It was time to get the day started. After cleaning up in the deluxe attached bathroom, Peri dressed, then headed downstairs. He found Devin, Bastian and Callan in the kitchen. Bastian was buckling Callan into a high chair. Mishu was parked underneath the chair, no doubt waiting for any food that might spill.

"Good morning, sleeping beauty," Devin said when he noticed Peri. "You're just in time for breakfast."

"It's not my fault. Your guest room is like a five-star suite. Is there anything I can do to help?"

"No, I got it. Just sit."

"It smells great," Peri said as he sat down.

"French toast."

"And sausage patties," Bastian added with a grin as he pulled a stack of plates from the cupboard.

"They have pork breakfast sausage on Dega?"

"No," Devin answered. "They're made from saki. We get them from a specialty shop in the Capital that sells Earth spices and other delicacies. They taste just like the real thing. Maybe even better. We get their bacon as well. It's really good."

"An Earth specialty shop. And I don't think I've ever heard someone classify bacon as a delicacy. Who would have thought?"

Once Devin finished cooking, Bastian insisted he sit.

After breakfast, they went outside into the backyard. Devin snagged a blanket from a tall wicker basket as he walked through the porch door.

Peri shielded his hand over his eyes as he walked with Devin toward the lake. "How long did it take you to get used to the sky?"

"Hmm? Oh, the purple hue? I don't even notice it anymore."

Peri glanced at Devin's belly. He sure had gotten used to a lot since moving here.

Once they reached the lake, Peri took the blanket from Devin and spread it on the grass. He helped Devin squat down, then sit. Devin placed his hand on his distended stomach.

"Wow," Peri wondered as he looked around the yard. He'd never seen so much grass, plus all the trees, and the lake. Peri noticed a hammock hanging between two trees.

Callan and Mishu chased each other, running in circles around the yard. Callan giggled up a storm. His face was all smiles.

It was all so magical. He took in a deep breath and let it out slowly. The air was warm. It smelled... *clean.*

Peri really envied Devin. Growing up in an orphanage having nothing, he always had big dreams about what his life *should* be like. None of those dreams ever came true, though. Devin had always been a realist, but here he was living his dream.

Devin breathed in and let it out in a sigh. "This is my favorite spot. If I'm ever stressed, sitting by the lake always calms me."

"I can imagine…"

"That's Besh's house across the lake." Devin pointed to a home on the opposite shore. "He's never home, though."

Peri shot Devin a sideways glance. Why would he bring up Beshel? Did he think Peri would want to know, or even care where that man lived?

They sat for a while longer until Peri's comPad interrupted the silence. It was Aron Adler. Peri needed to take the call, but he didn't want to tell Devin about the baby. He wasn't ready to have that conversation just yet.

"Hello?"

"Hi Peri. It's Aron Adler."

"Hi, Aron. I'm sitting here with Devin."

Peri held his comPad so that Aron could see both men.

"Hi, Aron." Devin waved. "It's good to see you."

Peri cleared his throat. "So… are you calling about the *medicine* I asked you about?"

"Uh, yes, of course. I'm at the Degan Science Institute. Check in with the Exobiology Department."

"I'll be there this afternoon."

Peri hung up his phone.

"Medicine?" Devin queried. "Is everything okay?"

Peri waved his hand dismissively. "It's fine. I got some motion sickness on the way here."

"If you're sure… Bastian has to go into the city for work. He can take you, if you'd like. God, I'd love to go with you to see Aron, but I can't today. The doctor is coming out to the house for my check-up. Bastian has him coming out once a week." Devin rolled his eyes. "It's a little much."

"It's only because he loves you."

A smile spread across Devin's mouth, and it lit up his entire face. "Yeah."

* * * *

Bastian dropped Peri off in front of the Degan Science Institute.

The building was architecturally different than most of the other buildings Peri had seen so far. Instead of stone, the institute was nearly all glass and metal. Made up of a trio of cylindrical towers, the middle column was smaller than the other two. Tubes connected the three towers at various floors, letting people walk between them without going all the way to the ground floor. All three towers shared a common main floor lobby.

The building reminded Peri of one of those lucky bamboo plants they had on the counter at his favorite Chinese restaurant back on Earth. Only made of glass. And bigger. A lot bigger.

"Thank you for the ride," Peri said as he got out of the hover car.

"Of course. Are you sure you'll be fine until I pick you up?"

"Yeah, I'll be fine. It's just a few hours."

"Okay. Call me or Devin if you need anything before then."

"Thanks, Bastian."

"Any time, Peri. Devin is so happy you're here, and so am I."

Knowing that Bastian meant every word, Peri couldn't help but smile. "Thanks. I'm glad I'm here, too."

Peri watched Bastian drive off before he turned toward the Institute. He walked up the sidewalk toward the center of the bottom floor. Entering the lobby, he looked around, easily locating the security guard station.

The guard sat behind a wide desk. He stared at a computer screen, and didn't look up when Peri cleared his throat. "Hello."

"Do you have an appointment?" the guard asked, his eyes never leaving the computer.

"Well, no… I'm supposed to meet Dr. Aron Adler here."

After a moment of typing, the guard replied, "There is no Dr. Aron Adler employed here."

"Sorry. He's a guest of the Exobiology Department."

"One moment. Have a seat."

Deciding to ignore the rude security guard, Peri sat down in one of the lobby chairs. Built for a Degan-sized humanoid, it felt too big. Peri's feet didn't even touch the ground, unless he stretched and pointed his toes. It made him feel like a kid. It made him feel uneasy.

He also noticed he was getting many sideways glances from the people coming and going. Nearly all Degan, Peri felt like an alien freak.

When Aron emerged from one of the elevators, Peri let out a breath of relief. He pushed out of the chair and walked over to greet the scientist he'd come to think of as a friend.

"It's good to see you, Peri."

"You, too." Peri shook Aron's outreached hand. "And Devin sends his regards."

A Degan male wearing a baby blue lab coat stood with Aron. Unlike many of the Degans he'd seen around the city, he didn't wear a skirt. He wore a dark blue cotton jumpsuit, similar to the kind he'd seen nurses wear back home. His brown hair was frazzled and uncombed.

The Degan gave Peri an awkward smile and held out his hand. "I am Doctor Neolin Thorsel. I am an exobiologist with the Degan Science Institute. I have been entrusted with the care of our"—he glanced around, then lowered his voice—"little friend."

Peri shook Doctor Thorsel's hand. "It's nice to meet you. I'm Peri McSmith."

"Why don't we go up to my lab where we can talk freely?"

"Okay."

"Let's get you checked in first."

Peri followed Thorsel over to the guard desk. Once Peri gave a hand scan identification, he received a guest ID badge to wear around his neck. He followed Thorsel and Aron to the middle tower's elevator banks. They rode up to the twelfth floor.

Everything was so white and sterile. Scientists dressed similarly to Thorsel roamed the halls, their faces buried in their comPads. Most of the labs had windows you could see into from the hall, though some had polarized glass, obstructing passersby from looking in.

When they reached Thorsel's lab, he scanned his hand for ID, then let Peri and Aron inside.

The lab was straight up creepy.

One wall contained shelves of books, from floor to ceiling. Many of them looked worn and ancient. Peri figured everything would be digitized on the network now, but apparently Thorsel was old school. *Really* old school.

There was a shelf filled with glass jars with unidentified bits and pieces and parts floating inside.

And then there were glass aquariums filled with bugs and rodents and all kinds of creepy things.

Gross.

A violent shudder ran down Peri's back. He swiped at his arm where he was sure a spider was crawling.

Covering his mouth with a hand, Aron snickered.

"I apologize," Thorsel said. "My methods are a bit unconventional. Come. This way."

He led Peri to the far corner where an ultra-modern computer workstation was set up. The portable cryo-freezer was connected to the computer. Next to the freezer was another similar chamber, this one empty.

"We're running some tests to make sure everything is good before we deactivate the cryo-freezer. Then we'll transfer it to the stage one incubator."

Peri leaned in and peered at the bundle of cells. "He's okay, though?"

"Perfectly fine." Thorsel gave Peri a toothy grin.

Aron offered Peri a chair. "Have a seat, Peri."

"Thank you."

"So, have you given any more thought as to who the sire might be?"

Peri schooled his features. "No."

Thorsel hummed. "Looking over the data, I believe whoever it is, he is related to Bastian Drago."

Peri cleared his throat. "Really?"

The Degan scientist nodded. "Oh, yes. The genetic markers are thirteen-point-eight percent similar. In fact, Aron and I have hypothesized that something about this family's DNA interacts with humans in a particular way that makes *this* possible." Thorsel indicated the embryo.

The lab door opened with a swoosh and Doctor Thorsel quickly rose to his feet. "Director Zorn. I wasn't expecting you."

Director Zorn was an older Degan. His hair was longer than most Degan males Peri had seen. Streaked generously with grey, it was pulled back into a ponytail at the base of his neck.

"I was looking for your guest, actually." He turned toward Aron. "Doctor Adler, we've received word that the *Cassini* is scheduled for departure. If you would please leave your badge at the guard's station when you leave. Thank you."

The director gave Peri a curious glance before turning and leaving the lab.

"Well, I guess that's my cue." With a frown, Aron pushed to his feet.

Peri stood and gave Aron a quick hug. "Thank you for everything."

"Of course. You keep in touch. Don't hesitate to call me if you need anything."

"I will."

Thorsel gave Aron a vigorous handshake. "It was good seeing you again, Aron. Let me walk you down." He stopped and turned to Peri. "Will you be fine on your own here for a few moments?"

Peri nodded. "I'll be okay."

When the two scientists left, Peri sat in the chair and stared at his baby.

* * * *

Beshel re-read the intelligence report a second time. In a show of good faith, Union Security had provided Beshel's agency with the data retrieved by the *Cassini* crew during their last mission.

According to this report, the human father of the embryo retrieved from XP-8460 was Perin McSmith, the friend of his nephew's human husband. The human subject was designated only as *H2* in the data files. The Degan sire, designation *D2*, was still unknown.

He'd met Perin McSmith once, back on Earth. He liked to be called Peri. While quite attractive, he was a tad... *fragile*. Naturally, if Beshel had taken him, he would likely have crushed the little human, or split him in half.

Beshel was supposed to help him pack Devin's belongings. He could remember meeting Peri at Devin's apartment, but when he thought back on that night, his memories were fuzzy.

Reaching back and rubbing his neck, Beshel began to pace.

Peri had... *procreated* with someone to produce the offspring. Not someone. A Degan. He'd let some other Degan fuck him. Was it one of the men on his team? Barlan maybe?

The sound of plastic crunching stopped him in his tracks. He looked down to see his fingers had cracked the front of the comPad's screen. Using every ounce of strength, he tossed the pad against the wall. It snapped and fell to the floor, the screen now broken and unlit. Beshel looked around the office, searching for something else to break, but stopped himself.

Why the hell did he care so much?

Chapter 6

"You didn't have to go to all this trouble."

Peri looked around and cringed. The back patio and yard of Devin's house were filled with Degans, relatives and family friends of Bastian. A tent was set up, and there was a table filled with a massive amount of food. There were these weird paper balloon things that had captured the attentions of Callan and one of his cousins, a little girl who looked like she was about his same age. Naturally, Bastian was close by, watching over the two toddlers. As was Mishu.

"What? Of course I did," Devin said. "You're new to the... well, to the *planet*, so it's only right we throw you a welcome party."

"I guess, but did you have to invite so many people? It's just... So much."

"You'll come to find Degans don't do *anything* small. They're all about big. Besides, maybe we can find you a man." Dev waggled his eyebrows. "A hot Degan man."

The last thing Peri needed right now was a man. Besides, who would want him when they discovered he had someone else's baby, even if it was grown in a test tube. "I don't need a man."

Dev narrowed his eyes suspiciously. "Okay, who are you and what have you done with Peri?"

"Dork."

"I did mention that Degan's are all about big, didn't I? And by *big*, I meant—"

"Slut."

"Oh, here come Bastian's parents. Let me introduce you."

An elderly Degan couple approached, walking arm in arm. Bastian's mother was very regal. While many of the women dressed in earth tones, her flowing dress was colorful, made of bright fuchsia, with a turquoise accent scarf. She wore no make-up, save for something that made her lips glossy, though her horns were quite smooth and had a subtle pink shade to them, as if they'd been... manicured, for a lack of a better word. Her tail swung behind her as she walked, the poofy fur at the end styled as meticulously as the rest of her. That was something Peri had noticed about Degan females. They had tails; the men did not.

With honey-colored fur and emerald green eyes, his sire looked like an older version of Bastian. Or perhaps a bigger, taller version of Beshel.

A spontaneous flash of a memory sailed across Peri's mind. *Peri held out an egg roll. Beshel leaned in. Their eyes locked as he aggressively—yet somehow still sensually—took a bite.*

"Nydia and Dashel Drago, this is Peri."

Jerking away from the inappropriate thought, Peri smiled and held out his hand. "It's a pleasure to meet you."

When Nydia bypassed his hand and pulled him in for a hug, Peri was caught off guard. "Oh!"

Once she was done, she passed him to Dashel, who also gave him a welcoming hug, one that was hard enough to nearly squeeze the air from his lungs.

"It's a pleasure to finally meet you, dear," Nydia said as she took one of his hands and held it between hers. "Devin has told us so much about you. I am positive you will love living here as well."

"Well, thank you. You didn't have to go through all this trouble."

Nydia sniffed. "Nonsense. You are Devin's brother. That makes you family."

"Oh." Peri pressed his lips together. He could feel tears welling in his eyes, and the last thing he wanted to do was burst into tears. "Thank you."

Dashel reached out and rubbed Peri's arm. "Of course. You let us know if you need anything. Anything at all."

* * * *

Beshel wasn't sure why he was here. Nydia loved any excuse for a party and a chance to bring the entire family together. Normally, he would've loved the chance to gather with his brother Dashel and the family, but for some reason the thought of seeing Peri made him uneasy.

Peri looked out of place among the family. He looked uncomfortable, both in the way he was dressed and with all of the attention.

Unlike Devin, he was dressed in Earth-style clothing. He wore a pair of tight denim pants and a black cotton short-sleeved shirt. When he moved just right, the hem of the shirt rode up enough to expose the flatness of his stomach, along with the top of his undergarments' waistband.

Beshel involuntarily licked his lips and had to swallow as his mouth began to fill with saliva.

From a distance, he watched one of Dashel's acquaintances talking with Peri. The man was standing awfully close. And what was he doing here anyway? He wasn't related to anyone; he wasn't family.

"Little brother, what are you growling at?"

Beshel cringed. He hadn't been aware of Dashel even approaching him, let alone the growls that had escaped his throat.

"Don't call me 'little brother'."

"My, someone's testy." Dashel chuckled with amusement. "It wouldn't have anything to do with our guest of honor now, would it?"

Beshel scoffed. "Of course not."

"Ah. Well, it looks like Grobel is chatting him up. He'd be a good catch for Peri, being a corporate executive and all. And I hear he— Oh, there's that noise again. Perhaps you should get that checked out."

"You know nothing."

Not wanting to hear his brother's grating voice any longer, Beshel stalked away. He found himself wandering close to Peri and that slimy Grobel. *He's probably the one who knocked him up.* Beshel sipped his ale as he pretended not to listen to the two talk. Grobel spent the precious time bragging about his material possessions, his job and the government contract he'd just secured.

Beshel cursed under his breath when Dashel walked up to Peri. "Excuse me, Peri? Do you mind if I borrow Grobel for a second?"

"Of course not," he answered with a smile.

As Dashel walked away with Grobel, he shot Beshel a look, tipping his head back toward Peri.

That meddling old...

"Hi."

Beshel turned toward that soft, melodic voice to find Peri waving at him.

"Hi," Beshel responded in turn. After an awkward moment, he closed the distance. "How have you been?"

"Fine. You?"

"Fine."

After an awkward moment of silence, Peri finally asked, "So... Catch any bad guys since I last saw you?"

"My investigation is still ongoing."

"Well, I'm sure Devin and Bastian appreciate all that you're doing. So, maybe we could grab lunch or dinner sometime."

"That would be nice."

A sly little smile spread across his face. "You don't know of any Chinese restaurants do you?"

Beshel shrugged. "I don't know. I've never been to one before."

Peri frowned. "Yes, you have. In Devin's apartment. Chopsticks." He pinched his fingers together.

Beshel rubbed the back of his neck. He tried to think back on that night. He hadn't had dinner with Peri, and he hadn't had Chinese, chopsticks, or whatever it was. "I don't think so. You must have me confused with another Degan."

Peri actually had the nerve to look offended. "Just forget it."

"Fine."

"Bastian and Devin make such a beautiful family. I'm sure it must be wonderful to find your soulmate, uh, bondmate."

Beshel shrugged "Eh."

"What do you mean 'eh'?"

"You don't actually believe in that nonsense? It's a trite relic from an era of superstitions and charlatans."

"God, you are so rude." Peri rolled his eyes. "I gotta go."

Beshel watched him leave. He tried to resist, but his eyes wandered down to Peri's ass. What a nice ass it was. The gentlemanly thing to do would be to go after him and apologize.

Once again, he didn't hear his brother approach. Dashel sighed. "Well, that could have gone... better."

"Shut up," Beshel muttered before walking off in the opposite direction.

Chapter 7

Peri picked up a powder blue onesie from the rack.

The front was printed with a round cartoon banti face: big eyes, smiling widely, with its tongue hanging out. It was so damn cute, Peri wanted to eat it up. He wondered what his baby boy would look like wearing it, and he couldn't help but smile.

Devin looked over Peri's shoulder. "Oh my gosh, that's adorable! But it's way too small for Callan. He's in toddler 1X now." He looked down at Callan, who sat in his stroller contentedly eating a shortbread type of cookie, leaving a massive amount of crumbs all over the place. Callan looked up at his daddy with his big green eyes and smiled. "Besides, we're supposed to be looking for girl clothes." Devin walked around the racks, flipping through the various articles, looking for the perfect outfit. "After we're done here, we should go shopping for you."

Giving one last look, Peri reluctantly hung the onesie back on its hanger. "Me?"

"Yeah. We should get you some Degan clothes. You don't want to keep wearing your old jeans and T-shirts do you?"

"What's wrong with my jeans?" Peri swung around and looked at himself in one of the store's full-length mirrors. "They make my ass look good."

Devin laughed. "If you say so."

"I do say so. Besides, I don't think I'm ready to wear a skirt." Peri pointed toward Devin.

"I didn't either, but, damn, is it comfortable."

Peri walked around another rack, sifting through the clothes.

"Grobel called me last night."

Devin perked up. "Really? Which one is that? The business executive?"

"Yeah. He wanted to take me to dinner."

"So, when are you going?"

Peri shrugged. "I don't think I'm into him. I mean, he's kind of a douche. He kept bragging about his house and cars."

Devin laughed.

"Oh, yes," Peri continued, mimicking Grobel's voice and inflections. "He has his eye on this *fabulous* new shuttle, what with his new contract and all. Exclusive contracts with the Degan Armed Forces can be very lucrative, didn't you know."

"Ew. Ditch that bozo."

"I know, right?"

After baby shopping, they stopped by another store to pick up some items for Peri. Devin insisted he get a kilt; he'd need it for dressing up. Peri wasn't so sure. He did like the tops, though. They went well with his jeans.

By the time they were finished, Peri was ready to head back home.

Devin pointed down the street. "Across the square is that specialty shop I told you about. Let's stop in real quick. I've been craving chocolate, and almond bars, and Oreos."

"So, Oreos are a delicacy too?"

"They are here," he said with a grin.

As they approached the shop, Peri was surprised at how popular the place was. There were several Degans standing outside, a group of men and a couple of women. Some of them carried handwritten signs. Ah, they were clerks trying to draw in the customers.

"Go home, off-worlder!" one of the men shouted as he pounded on the front door with a hand-held metal canister.

Devin and Peri froze. *Okay, definitely not store clerks, and definitely not customers.* In fact, the store looked like it was closed for business.

Using the canister, the protester began spraying the front window with graffiti. The crude drawings started to take on a decidedly obscene shape.

He was cheered on by the others. They waved their signs as they chanted in unison.

One of the protesters noticed Devin and Peri. "Off-worlders! Human trash!"

After hearing the first man shout, the entire crowd turned toward them. Abandoning their original target, they directed their hate towards the humans.

"Go back to Earth, humans, and take your half-breed abomination with you!" The man threw the paint canister, and it landed in front of Callan's stroller, banging against the wheel.

Peri gasped in horror.

Devin leaned down and plucked Callan from the stroller. He pulled him tight to his chest and turned the boy's head into his shoulder, shielding him from the men and women who continuously hurled insults that got louder and nastier.

They closed in, shouting and waving their signs. As their taunts rose in volume and they moved in closer, Callan began to cry.

Peri wrapped his arms around Devin and Callan, and turned them around, but not before shooting a death glare at the assholes. "The whole lot of you can go to hell and fuck off!"

Devin's entire body shook as he and Peri fled across the square. Peri was shaking, too; not because he was afraid, but because he was pissed off. How dare those people talk to Devin and Callan like that!

"I've never seen anything like that before," Devin said quietly, his voice trembling. "No one has ever spoken to Callan like that. Not in all the time we've lived here." He clutched his crying boy as tears fell down his cheeks. "We left the stroller…"

"I think we should call Bastian." Peri pulled out his comPad and scrolled through the contacts. When the call activated, he gave Bastian a quick rundown of what happened, and then handed the pad to Devin.

Was this what it was going to be like for Peri and his baby? Only Peri didn't have a husband or family here. There'd be no one to turn to when a mob of angry Degans came after him.

Maybe this wasn't an ideal place to raise a child after all....

* * * *

The hover-taxi dropped Peri off in front of the science institute. As he got out of the car, he looked around, making sure there weren't any protesters around. He reached into his pocket and felt for the tiny can of heat-spray Bastian had given him. It had been a couple of days since the incident at the square, but Peri was still freaked out about it.

He hurried into the lobby, wanting to get off the street. After asking for Dr. Thorsel by name at the guard station, things went more smoothly than his last visit.

Still, he couldn't help but be anxious while waiting for the scientist to come down to the lobby. He sat in the waiting area, swinging his foot a hundred times a minute. Maybe he was being paranoid, but it seemed like everyone was watching him. He waited for someone to yell at him, to tell him to go home. God, if they knew what he was doing here, they'd probably shit a brick.

"Peri," Dr. Thorsel said with a wide grin. He held out a hand and helped Peri out of his chair. "It's good to see you. Follow me." A hand moved to Peri's back, leading him toward the elevator banks.

Peri followed Thorsel into his laboratory. Ignoring all the old books and creepy jars, he went straight to the back.

The embryo had been removed from cryo-sleep and was now in an incubation chamber. It all sounded scary and dangerous to Peri, despite Thorsel's constant assurances. He couldn't wait to see it in person.

When he peered into the incubator's clear window, he let out a startled gasp.

The embryo was twice as big as the last time he'd seen it! "What happened?"

"Its size? Now that it's been moved to the stage one incubator, it's growing at an accelerated pace."

"That's not bad for it?"

"No. This procedure is done quite frequently. Many couples who are unable to have children naturally take advantage of this technology. It's very safe and has been in use for decades."

"Oh. It's still so little, though."

Peri peered in closer. It still didn't look like anything remotely humanoid. In fact, it looked like an overgrown, gelatinous peanut to Peri. He didn't comment on this aloud, not wanting to sound stupid in front of the scientist.

"He is at the stage where his central nervous system is developing."

"Do you think it hurt him?" Peri wondered out loud.

"Did what hurt?"

"The experiments they did on him. The cells they took."

"No," Thorsel quietly answered.

Peri sniffled and straightened up, and turned to face Thorsel. "So, you said this is a stage one incubator? Are there more stages?"

"Yes. Once he has reached the point where he could survive outside the host parent's body, he'll be moved to a stage two maturation unit, where he'll grow until he can function on his own."

"Thank you, doctor, for everything you're doing. I appreciate it."

Dr. Thorsel gave Peri a smile and patted his shoulder. "You're quite welcome. I have some work to do, but you are welcome to stay as long as you'd like."

"Thanks."

Peri sat with the embryo for quite a while longer. Dr. Thorsel continued on with his research, checking in on Peri from time to time, but mostly he left Peri alone with the baby, and his thoughts.

The chiming of his comPad interrupted Peri's daydream.

Ugh. If that insufferable bore Grobel was calling him again, he was going to have to cuss him out. Looking at the screen, he was so startled he almost didn't answer in time.

Beshel Drago was the last person he'd expected to be calling him.

* * * *

Beshel knew his brother was right, but that didn't make it any easier to swallow. He'd been extremely rude to Peri at the party last weekend, and the young human did not deserve it.

For the life of him, he did not understand why he'd acted that way. He was normally calm and cool. Level-headed. Something about the man just... got to him. It made him act stupid. That was all the more reason to stay away.

But not until he apologized.

Speaking of apologies, it was those fucking xenophobic protesters who should be apologizing. Until now they just looked like radicals, a handful of lunatics protesting foreign festivals and off-world specialty stores. But recently, some of their protests had escalated into vandalism and violence.

Dashel had the Capital City police force take care of this particular group, but they had already scared Devin, Peri and Callan. If Dashel had his way, the entire lot would be taken out and shot for frightening his grandson and making him cry. He was fiercely protective of the little boy. But the governor of the Capital province couldn't very well do that. Beshel, on the other hand, had contacts which could easily dispatch them, and make it look like an accident.

As soon as Dashel had told him what happened, Beshel placed a call to Agent Barlan to have them put on the bureau's watch-list.

Picking up his comPad, Beshel placed the call. It took so long to connect, Beshel was ready to cancel, and then Peri's apprehensive face appeared on his screen.

"Yes?"

"Hello, Peri."

"Can I help you with something?"

Ouch. That was cold.

Beshel cleared his throat. "I wanted to apologize for my behavior at your party the other day. I was… frustrated… and I took it out on you."

"Oh." The little man was stunned speechless. He stared back at Beshel with big brown eyes. "Oh. Uh, well, thank you."

"You're welcome."

"So does that mean we're on for dinner?"

"Well… sure."

Chapter 8

Peri looked around the restaurant. He wasn't sure he was in the right place. He thought Beshel would've chosen a place in the Capital, but this place was a good ways outside the city. It wasn't too crowded, and it was dimly lit. The smells coming from the kitchen made his mouth water, though.

There was a possibility that Beshel was the sire of his baby. If that was the case, Peri needed to make sure they could at least be civil around each other. Besh inviting him to dinner to apologize for being an ass was a good first step.

He found Beshel, hand raised over his head, at a table in the back corner.

Peri made his way to Beshel's table and sat down. The over-sized chair scooted against the wooden floor, the noise echoing far louder than he would have liked, as he tried to shimmy it closer to the table.

"Interesting choice," he said when he finally got settled. "I'm not sure if you're trying to be romantic, or if you're making sure you're not seen with me in public."

"I chose this place because they make excellent food. I have no ulterior motives." Beshel adjusted his silverware on the table, making sure the two forks and the knife were lined up precisely, all equidistant from each other and his appetizer plate, centered at the middle.

"So a combination of both: romantic *and* discreet." Peri reached over and pushed the middle fork out of alignment.

Beshel shook his head slowly as he moved the fork back. "Sometimes I just do not know what to make of you."

"That's a good thing, Besh."

Peri picked up his menu and read through it. They had cuisine from all over the planet, but they also had a nice selection of off-world dishes. The Regulan meatloaf sounded intriguing, but Peri decided to go for a Degan entrée instead.

After putting in their order, they made small talk. Mostly about the weather this time of year. A little bit about Devin. Anything they could do to dance around what was really going on.

When their food finally arrived, Peri was relieved. He wouldn't have to force himself to come up with more inane conversation while they ate.

* * * *

Beshel had never seen anyone eat as sensually as Perin McSmith. Just watching his fork disappear into his mouth, with a hint of tongue, made his cock hard. It was a good thing the table wasn't see-through. He knew he was sporting a hefty bulge in his leather pants.

"Mmm," Peri moaned. His tongue slid his across lips. "This is really good. I might have to lick this sauce right from the plate. Want a bite?" Leaning over the table, he held his fork out toward Beshel. A smell wafted across the table. Something he'd never smelled before, but it was hauntingly familiar. He couldn't help but take a deep whiff, drawing the scent deep into his lungs. His cock lurched in his pants.

Peri held out the egg roll. Beshel leaned in. With eyes locked on Peri, he bit down, taking nearly the entire roll into his mouth. Before pulling away, he swirled his tongue across Peri's fingers. It was blatantly and aggressively sexual. Judging from Peri's quickened breathing and dilated pupils, he was very aware of it.

"What's wrong?"

Beshel blinked rapidly. He focused his eyes on Peri. "Nothing."

"Did you remember something?"

Why was he remembering a fragment from his dream? It was as if he could taste the egg roll. He knew for certain he'd never had one before, but he could taste the cabbage, sprouts and shrimp. He could feel the sizzling heat of the fried wrapper on his tongue. He swallowed, trying to get rid of it.

And how did Peri know?

"I don't know what you're talking about."

"Uh-huh." Peri ate the bite of food off his fork. While staring into Besh's eyes, he swiped his tongue along the tines, cleaning it of sauce.

"Fuck," Beshel muttered under his breath as he squirmed in his chair. His erection was really starting to bother him. Too bad he hadn't worn a kilt today. He could use the extra breathing room right about now. Unable to take the aching discomfort any longer, he reached down and gripped his hard-on through his pants, attempting to shift it into a more comfortable position. It didn't help.

Peri's nostrils flared. "So, is there a place close by where we could go?" he whispered as he watched Beshel manipulate his cock. Peri's fingernails scraped the tablecloth, and he balled his hand into a fist. He looked up at Beshel, his pupils blown wide open. Nostrils flared once more as he licked his lips.

Beshel stood and flagged down the waiter.

* * * *

Beshel was unable to resist Peri. The little human was triggering all of his fetishes.

Those little sounds he made as Beshel kissed and sucked on his neck would be his undoing. Those little gasps as Beshel trailed his lips over the nape of his neck.

He wanted to taste Peri, taste all of him, but he was distracted by the hard little nubs on his chest. He'd never seen a male with nipples before. Yes, he'd had sex with a human man once before, but it was quick and dirty, years ago. Beshel had met the human soldier on a starbase while working on a case. The human was bold in his flirting, and Beshel gave the man what he asked for. They hadn't even made it to the bed, or bothered to undress. He took the Union officer from behind, right there at the front door of his assigned quarters.

But this was different.

There was the same sense of urgency, but it wasn't about filling an animalistic need. He wanted to give Peri pleasure.

The smooth skin fascinated Beshel, and he wondered if the lack of body fur made Peri feel chilly. Besides his head, the only places Peri had any sort of hair were under his arms and around his penis. The dark curls there contrasted sharply with the pink flesh that arose there, throbbing and straining, as if trying to reach out to Beshel.

As he stroked his hands up and down, Peri's body quivered, and goose bumps erupted. It was damn heady knowing he could cause such a reaction.

Beshel worked the nipple with his tongue, alternating quick flicks with leisurely swirls. When he pulled back, the hard nub glistened with his saliva. Beshel blew a puff of air across it, and Peri moaned softly.

Peri's hands moved to Beshel's head. The slightest of pressure was accompanied by an inhale of breath. Beshel knew what Peri wanted, but he wasn't ready for that yet. He had another nipple to taste. As he worked the nub, Peri moved continuously beneath him, pushing his hips up, pressing his cock against Beshel, rubbing it into his fur.

"Please," Peri whispered.

Unable to deny Peri's sweet pleas, Beshel moved down until he hovered over his prize. Taking a moment to look at it, Beshel marveled at its beauty. Running his hand down it, the silky foreskin retreated, exposing the glossy slick head, reddened by the blood pulsing through it. Letting rest against his palm, Beshel admired its thickness, how perfectly proportioned it was to Peri's body size.

A perfect mouthful.

He effortlessly swallowed the shaft to the base as it throbbed against his tongue. The dark tufts of hair tickled his lips. Applying suction, he raised his head until the crown popped free. Peri's cock leaked the sweetest of juices and Beshel swirled his tongue around it, capturing the flavor.

Wanting more, he dove back down, sucking and tonguing the human. Over and over he did this, torturing Peri, who shuddered and trembled beneath him.

Beshel wanted to take his time, but the need to taste Peri overtook him. The boy's smells and sounds were fuel to Beshel's fire. Using his mouth, he relentlessly drove Peri to the brink.

Further down between Peri's legs, a musky scent called to

Beshel. He ran a finger across the hidden entrance, and Peri bucked beneath him.

"Besh." The whisper was urgent. His hand lightly tugged at one of Beshel's horns. "Besh, I'm gonna come. I can't— Oh, please, don't stop!"

The feel of Peri's fingers on his horn made his cock jerk, throwing him into a frenzy. Growling in his throat, Beshel increased his urgency, sucking harder and bobbing his head faster. Peri began to writhe on the bed, his hips raising up, driving his shaft into the back of Beshel's mouth.

And then Beshel got his prize.

Peri let out a stifled cry, which morphed into an unabashed moan, as he began to spurt into Besh's throat. Backing off until the head rested on his tongue, Beshel sucked and tongued it, tasting every remaining burst. The taste and smell of Peri's cum sent Beshel into overdrive.

His lips still dripping with Peri's release, Beshel climbed up Peri's body until he was lying over him, their hips pressed together. Grinding his swollen cock into Peri's body, Beshel looked down at the man trapped beneath him.

He leaned down for a kiss, but something stopped him.

The look in Peri's eyes.

* * * *

Déjà vu. That was the only way Peri could describe it. And by the way Beshel froze, he sensed it as well.

"Have we…"

Beshel shook his head. "No."

"Are you sure?"

Peri looked up at Beshel and studied him. It wasn't just the way he looked, but the way he felt on top of him, the way he smelled. It all seemed familiar.

While studying the Degan, Peri noticed a small heart-shaped mark on his left earlobe. He reached up and stroked his thumb across the red flesh. "What's this?"

"A birthmark," he replied softly.

"It looks like a heart."

"Actually, it looks more like a raka bean."

"I suppose that may be true, but a heart would be more romantic. So for future arguments, if you're ever naked and on top of someone, and they comment on it, a *heart* would be the way to go."

But enough talking.

Peri reached between their bodies and gripped Beshel's engorged cock with both of his fists. Once again that feeling of déjà vu seeped in. Ignoring it, Peri lifted his head and met Beshel's lips as he began to move his hands.

He used his hands to urge Beshel forward.

Immediately getting the hint, Beshel crawled up, straddling Peri's body. One more push forward sent the head of his cock to the back of Peri's mouth.

Peri moaned, his mouth stuffed full. The vibrations traveled through Besh's shaft and he felt Beshel tremble.

Peri's hands moved to Beshel's ass. Applying pressure, he got Besh to move.

Beshel pulled back and thrust. He fucked Peri's mouth, clearly trying to keep his motions shallow. Peri appreciated that. No way could he take that monster into his throat, and he certainly didn't want his obituary to read that he died chocking on a dick.

Peri used his hands to massage Beshel's furred assed cheeks and the back of his thighs. It wasn't long before he figured out that Beshel liked a strong suction. He used his tongue to flutter back and forth, swirling around the head when he could.

Beshel looked down and met Peri's eyes. A pained expression swiftly took over his face. As the Degan's mouth hung open, his eyes went wide just before they rolled back into his head.

Beshel roared. His body bucked uncontrollably.

The sweltering helmet swelled against Peri's tongue. His mouth was abruptly filled with scalding liquid.

Peri swallowed.

And none too soon, because Besh kept coming and coming. Finally, the furry alien let out a rush of breath and collapsed forward, his arms clutching the bed's headboard, holding his weight back.

* * * *

Peri stared up at the ceiling, his breathing still coming fast and shallow.

He hadn't meant to do that. Even before they started, Peri knew it was a mistake. The Spaceport Prime operating system had more emotion than Beshel Drago, who was currently holed up in his bathroom. Hiding like a bitch.

The view of him walking away was not bad, though. And he'd discovered that Beshel had a docked tail.

Despite having been pretty much ditched, he had to admit it was *good*. Peri wasn't as experienced as he led others to believe, but he knew what he'd just done—and had done to him—was once in a lifetime, out of this world, amazing.

Sure his jaw was a bit sore, and Beshel had nearly drowned him, but it was worth it. Raising his hands over his head, Peri stretched. He rolled over and buried his face in Beshel's pillow. It was slightly damp with sweat, but it smelled freaking fantastic.

Something tickled the end of Peri's nose.

Pulling back, he focused his eyes on a long, thick strand of honey-colored hair.

Peri plucked the hair from the pillow, twirled it into a ball, and hid it away.

Chapter 9

Beshel stood outside the Degan Science Institute, watching.

Scientists moved in and out of the lobby. All of the men and women he'd seen so far had been Degan, most of them dressed in thin woven fabric jumpsuits with lab coats. A handful of security officers, civilians who functioned as armed guards for the Institute, patrolled the grounds. He'd also seen one high-ranking member of the Degan Armed Forces.

Nothing out of the ordinary.

His investigation had led him here, to a Dr. Neolin Thorsel. One of the Degan Federation's leading exobiologists, Thorsel was the natural choice for taking custody of the hybrid recovered from the destroyed research colony on planet XP-8460.

It was his hope the scientist would be able to put him on the right path, to the men who'd created the hybrid and then perfected the genetic manipulations based on their creation. Even if he wasn't involved, surely he knew of others in his field who might have either the expertise or the ambition to do such things.

Imagine his surprise when Peri McSmith showed up, and met with Thorsel. The two men seemed awfully cozy. Yes, Peri was the biological father of the hybrid, but Beshel was unaware that Peri knew of this, and had taken an interest in it. Or perhaps he was interested in Thorsel.

Standing off to the side, hidden behind a steel column, Beshel watched through the window as Thorsel led Peri to the elevators.

* * * *

"I can't believe how big it is already."

It now had tiny little nubs for limbs, and its shape was starting to form. *He* was definitely a humanoid, no longer… *peanutoid.*

"Yes, it's moved into the fetus stage now."

"He has eyes."

Peri stared at the tiny dots and wondered if he would have his brown eyes. Perhaps it would have the eyes of his sire, bright emerald green. Reaching into his pocket, he fingered the envelope. He wasn't sure if he should do this, but he had to know.

"Doctor Thorsel?"

Thorsel looked up from the microscope he had set up on his workstation. "Yes, Peri?"

Pulling the envelope from his pocket, he walked up to the doctor. "If I give you this, will you promise not to ask me any questions about it?"

Thorsel frowned, but took the envelope, and peeked inside. "Ah. This belongs to the sire?"

"Maybe... I'm not sure."

"Very well. It will only take a few minutes for the computer to break down the sample and analyze the results."

He left the room with the envelope, and Peri turned back toward the baby. Now that he had little eyes and little limbs, he couldn't help but think of it as a baby.

Thorsel returned several minutes later. He held out the envelope to Peri. "The results are in. This hair—"

Peri held his breath.

"—does indeed belong to the sire."

Peri felt the tears coming. His baby boy had been born in a test tube. He didn't even have a birthday. His father didn't know what he was doing, and his sire was... The whole situation was beyond frustrating. He certainly couldn't tell Beshel what was going on. He didn't know himself.

"I don't understand... We never..."

* * * *

Beshel started for the lobby door, then changed his mind. Part of him wanted to storm into the office and demand to know what was going on. The other part of him didn't want to know at all.

But this was part of his investigation. Degan citizens had been violated while creating those robotic abominations of nature. It was his duty to follow up on this lead. He could send Barlan in his place.

No. He was no coward.

Just as he was about to enter the building, his comPad beeped. Pulling the device from his pocket, he activated the call.

"Yes, Agent?"

Agent Barlan's face appeared on the screen. "Excuse the interruption, Chief, but you're going to want to hear this."

* * * *

"Here." Thorsel handed Peri a tissue. "Everything will be all right."

"How?" Peri sniffled, then blew his nose. "I feel all alone in this. I don't know what to do."

Thorsel dropped to a squat in front of Peri's chair and cradled his smaller hand in his. "You're not alone. You have friends and family here. Rely on them. And you know I will help you anyway I can."

Peri wiped at his eyes. "I'm sorry for getting emotional. I guess it's just been building up."

"It's understandable. I know I said I wouldn't ask questions, but I strongly suggest you tell the baby's sire. He has a right to know."

"It's just... really complicated. We don't have any kind of relationship, not really. We—"

The lab door opened with a swoosh. Two of the building's security guards entered, followed by Beshel Drago.

And he looked *pissed*.

He was dressed in his leather uniform, with his badge hanging around his neck. The portions of his face that weren't covered in fur had gone red. A vein throbbed on his forehead. His hands were balled into tight fists.

For a moment, Peri wondered if the man was angry enough to get violent with him.

"What have you done?" he roared.

Chapter 10

Peri gasped in horror when Beshel drew his weapon and pointed it at Doctor Thorsel.

"Back away from him," Beshel demanded.

"Beshel, please," Peri pleaded. "Calm down."

Doctor Thorsel rose slowly, with hands displayed open in front of him. "Whatever you think is going on—"

"Shut up." When Thorsel had moved far enough to satisfy him, Beshel stormed over to Peri, who instinctively moved in front of the incubator.

"Besh, please," Peri repeated.

Crowding into Peri's personal space, Beshel peered over his shoulder to look down into the device behind Peri's back. If there was a reaction to what he saw, Peri did not see it on the investigator's face. He stayed in that position for a moment longer, and Peri did not dare move.

Holstering his weapon, Beshel finally turned back to the guards. "I've got it from here."

One guard nodded after glancing at the other. "Yes, sir. We'll be right outside the lab if you need us."

"Thank you."

After the guards left the room, Beshel rubbed the back of his neck and began to pace. "Somebody better start explaining to me what the fuck is going on here."

Peri cringed at Beshel's demeanor. "I don't know what to say."

Thorsel dropped his hands and looked down at Peri. "I take it this is the sire then?"

Peri nodded.

Infuriated, Beshel's arm lashed out, pointing at the incubator. His voice climbed in volume. "Did you do this? Are you working with them?"

Peri vehemently shook his head. "Of course not! I would never do that. I'm just as much in the dark as you are."

"How did you get my semen?" he demanded.

Peri cringed, annoyed and grossed out at the same time. "I didn't get your... *semen*."

"I'm Dr. Thorsel, by the way." Thorsel stepped forward and held out his hand.

Beshel swung, his accusing finger now pointing at Thorsel's chest. "I know who you are."

"Then you have me at a disadvantage."

"Beshel Drago. Chief Investigator for the Degan Federation."

"Aah. Are you related to Bastian Drago?"

Beshel eyed the doctor suspiciously. "He's my nephew. Why?"

"As you know, Degan DNA tends to be aggressive when introduced into other species' bodies. I have a theory that something about the genetics in your family can alter human DNA in specific ways, as seen in your nephew's bondmate."

"I always thought the mutations were random. Are they not?"

"Somewhat, but we have seen instances where certain interactions have a chance of being passed down through the sire's genetic material. We could test the theory fairly easily."

"How?"

"I would need a sample from each of you." Thorsel glanced toward Beshel's groin, suggesting the type of sample he would need. "Once they are combined, finding the right accelerator should trigger the mutation and growth." Thorsel tapped his chin with his finger as he thought aloud. "I have a couple of pharmacological candidates in my lab that would possibly do the trick."

"That's not going to happen, Doctor. So, why don't you go sit your perverted ass down over there?"

"Agreed," Peri mumbled.

"I am only trying to help."

Once the doctor sat down at his workstation, Peri moved closer to Beshel, despite the man's growly attitude. In a low voice, he asked, "Do you... um, sometimes have dreams about us?"

Beshel became very uncomfortable. He shifted his weight between his feet and averted his eyes. "No."

"I sometimes do," Peri admitted. "I dream about us doing stuff that I don't think we ever did... but maybe we did." He glanced toward the incubator and lifted an eyebrow.

Beshel's face went red and he pressed his lips together. "I did not make love to you. Trust me, you would remember it."

Peri rolled his eyes and scoffed. "Conceited much? My point is, Casanova, that maybe someone did something to us. And they, you know, *collected our samples.*" Peri glanced at Doctor Thorsel.

Moving around Peri, Beshel placed himself between Peri and Thorsel. He leaned down and whispered so only Peri could hear. "Do you think he's involved?"

Peri thought for a moment. "I don't think so. At least not knowingly."

"I don't trust him."

Peri placed a hand on Beshel's chest. The large man stiffened at first, but then relaxed into Peri's touch. "I need you to find out how they did this." Again, he glanced down at the baby. *Their* baby.

Beshel moved back a step, causing Peri's hand to fall away.

"Of course. It's my job..." Beshel stood in place awkwardly for a moment before he took a step back. "I better get back to it."

Peri stopped Beshel before he left. "We should talk about *him.*" He directed his eyes toward the incubator.

Beshel nodded without looking at Peri. "Yes. Later."

He left the lab without another word.

* * * *

Beshel drove home on auto-pilot.

Once he reached home, he went straight for his gym. He stripped down, tossing his uniform to the side. Naked, he stormed over to his sparring dummy.

With a roar, he took an attack stance and slammed the dummy's head with his fist. Alternating fists and kicks, he beat the hell out of the fleshy replica, wishing it was each and every one of those scientists.

When he got a hold of them… they were going to wish they'd never set eyes on a Degan. He'd show them exactly why Degans were once feared across the galaxy as a warrior race. If they wanted to see a *beast*, he'd show them one.

They had violated him, taken his DNA without his permission. They'd used it to create those *things* on XP-8460… brainless automaton prototypes, grafting biological components onto their metal chassis.

And they had done the same to Peri. The sweet little human did not deserve it. And now Peri was growing emotionally attached to the specimen they'd synthesized. Who knew what they'd done to it, what it would become once it grew.

With renewed energy, he attacked the dummy once more. He didn't stop until the pain in his hands finally registered in his brain.

Looking down at his knuckles, he found them raw. Blood dripped down back of his hands onto the matted floor. His hands shook so hard, he balled them into fists, trying to stop it. Fresh jolts of pain shot up his arms.

Beshel threw his head back and screamed until he was hoarse.

* * * *

The sound of screaming jolted Peri awake so hard, he nearly fell out of the bed.

Tossing back the covers, he jumped out of bed and raced out of the room. Following the noise, he found himself at Devin's bedroom door.

Groaning in agony, Devin was bent in a half squat, clutching his belly. Bastian raced around the room, picking up a satchel and a bathrobe. He was wide-eyed and frantic.

"My true one, please hold on." Bastian helped Devin up to a standing position. The desperate worry on his face made Peri's heart skip a beat. Was something wrong?

"Is there anything I can do?" Peri asked.

Bastian slung the satchel over his shoulder, covered Devin with the robe, then scooped him up into his arms. "Can you please get Callan? We're going to the hospital right now."

"I can walk," Devin said, his voice sounding weak.

Peri nodded. "I can do that. We'll meet you downstairs."

He immediately went to Callan's bedroom. The boy was fast asleep in his bed, arms and legs tangled up around Mishu. As soon as Peri entered the room, Mishu's eyes darted open. The furball's eyes traced Peri's every move as he extracted Callan from the bed.

"Ugh, you're heavy."

Callan started to fuss, so Peri grabbed the blue blanket from the bed. After wrapping him up, he pulled him close to his chest to rest the boy's head on his shoulder. "Your daddy is having the baby. Are you ready to be a big brother?"

"No," was the sleepy reply.

Peri laughed softly. "Join the club."

After making a quick stop in the kitchen to grab a drink and a snack for Callan, Peri met Bastian and Devin outside at the hovercar.

Carefully, Bastian helped Devin into his seat. As he buckled him in, Devin cried out in pain once more.

Bastian drew in a breath. "Please." He pressed a kiss to Devin's forehead. "I need you to be okay. We all do."

Peri got Callan buckled in, then situated himself. Bastian took off before the door was even fully closed. Bastian turned back to Peri. "Thank you for taking care of Callan. You're a natural."

He smiled back at Bastian, not sure of what he'd done that

Bastian would say such a thing. Peri looked down at Callan. Buckled in his booster seat, the boy clutched his blanket with one hand. The two middle fingers of his other hand were firmly planted in his mouth. He was fast asleep.

They made it to the city in record time.

Devin was whisked away as soon as they pulled up to the hospital doors. Peri assured Bastian that he'd watch over Callan, and Bastian disappeared with his bondmate.

The waiting room was nice and comfortable, with big over-padded leather furniture. Peri sat with Callan while the boy ate his cookies. He wasn't sure how long he'd have to wait, but every minute seemed like an eternity.

He hadn't been there long when Bastian's parents arrived. They were then followed by Bastian's sisters. Elia brought a husband and gaggle of cousins for Callan to play with.

Nattie, Bastian's youngest sister, sat down next to Peri on the sofa. "We didn't get a chance to talk much at your party. I'm Nattie."

"I remember. Good to see you again." Peri held out his hand and Nattie shook it.

"So, what are your plans?"

Peri shrugged. "I don't really have anything set in stone. I told Devin that I'd help him with the babies. Beyond that, I haven't given it much thought." Not exactly true, but he wasn't about to spill his guts to someone who was pretty much a stranger.

"If you're looking for work, I'm sure someone knows someone who could help you out. We're a pretty big family. We have a lot of connections."

"I'm pretty sure I'll be up to my elbows with baby stuff."

"Well, if you ever need to get away from screaming, messy babies, give me a call. We can grab lunch and talk about my brother behind his back."

Peri laughed. "Okay, you got a deal."

"Say, let's go find the cafeteria and grab some food and drinks for everybody."

"Sure."

"We'll be right back," Nattie announced as they stood and left the room.

As they walked down the hall, Peri couldn't help but notice the way her tail swooped back and forth behind her. Though she was what Peri might consider short for a Degan, she was still taller than him by a few inches.

Curious, he reached out to touch the poofy furred tip. Just as he was about to make contact, it flitted away from his reach.

"Never touch a woman's tail." She stopped walking and looked at Peri with a raised brow. "Unless you're initiating a mating ritual." She stepped closer and blatantly sniffed the top of Peri's head.

As he stumbled back a step, Peri's mouth dropped open. "Uh, I, uh… No!"

Nattie burst into laughter. "I'm just kidding. You should see your face!"

Peri was mortified. "Oh my god."

"Relax. I don't think I'm your type." Nattie winked at him. She looped her arm around Peri's and they began walking again. "And it'd be like mating with family, especially since you're already screwing Uncle Besh."

Peri stopped in his tracks, jerking Nattie to a halt with his arm. "Wh— What?"

Nattie frowned. "Was that not the right word? Oh, wait, is it supposed to be a secret?"

"No, it's not a secret, because it's not true."

"Don't worry. Your secret's safe with me." She pursed her lips together and covered her mouth with her hand.

The rest of the way to the cafeteria and back, Nattie chatted incessantly. Whatever she said was completely lost on Peri. He was still trying to figure out why she would've thought that he and Besh were *screwing*.

They'd barely arrived back at the waiting room and passed out the drinks and snacks when Bastian walked in.

The room went silent as they waited to hear the news.

"Devin is fine. He's still sleeping off the anesthesia. The baby... she is fine."

Everyone let out a sigh of relief.

Bastian's parents were on their feet, hugging their son.

Peri smiled as he watched Bastian's relatives shower him with love. But the smile slipped away when he realized that he'd never have this moment. His baby boy had been "born" in a lab, and the only family he had was Peri.

* * * *

Peri was in the first group to see Devin, along with Nydia and Dashel.

Devin looked groggy and slightly out of it, but the smile on his face was radiant. He was propped up in a sitting position on the hospital bed. Bastian leaned over him, his arm holding up the back of Devin's head.

In Devin's arms, a baby girl was wrapped tight in a pink blanket.

Bastian pressed a kiss to the top of Devin's head. "Look what you made, my true one."

"Yeah," Devin grinned. "We did good."

Peri crowded around the bed with Bastian's parents to get a closer look at the baby.

"She's beautiful, Dev," Peri marveled.

Her face was still a touch on the red side, but she was gorgeous. Her hair was wet, but it was plentiful, the color of Bastian's fur. There were two nubby horns on top of her delicate head. She had big bright green eyes that darted back and forth, taking everything in. Beyond the eyes and horns, she looked so much like Devin that Peri was stunned. He leaned down and pressed a kiss to the side of Devin's head. "Congratulations, Dev. I'm so happy for you."

Nydia clutched at her chest. "She is the most precious thing I have ever seen."

Dashel wrapped his arm around his wife. He had a grin on his face a mile wide.

"Sire." Devin looked up at Bastian's father. "We have decided to name her Dasha... after you." Tears rolled down Devin's face. "You saved me. You made all this possible."

Dashel swallowed and started to speak, but had to stop to clear his throat. Even then, his voice still came out choked. "Thank you, my son." He tugged Devin's ear before leaning down to kiss his forehead.

He then did the same to Bastian, pulling Bastian into a bear hug. He did not let go.

Peri couldn't help but think about his baby, and how he'd never get to experience this like Devin did. And he hated himself for even thinking it.

Chapter 11

Barlan sat down in the chair opposite Beshel's desk.

Beshel was keenly aware of the man's presence, but he wasn't in the mood for a social visit. He kept his attention on his comPad. He had reports to read.

"So, how's it going, Chief?"

"Fine. Is there something I can help you with, Agent?" Beshel didn't look up.

"I'm just wondering if there's anything you'd like to talk about."

"No."

"I dropped a pretty big bombshell on you the other day."

Beshel started to grind his back teeth together, but stopped as soon as he realized he was doing it. He let out a slow breath in an attempt to calm himself. "If you're referring to the specimen, I don't have anything to say about it."

Barlan looked horrified. "*Specimen*? Is that what you're calling it?"

"And what would you call it?"

"I'd call it your *child*."

Barlan had the nerve to sound offended. *He* was the one who'd started this line of questioning. If anyone should be offended, it should be *Beshel*.

Beshel slammed the comPad on his desk. "I didn't have anything to do with the creation of it."

"Maybe not, but it's still your flesh and blood. But it's not just about you. The human—Peri—he is in the same situation as you. If you won't talk to me about it, then talk to him." Barlan stood. Before he left Beshel's office, he stopped and turned back. "And when I say *talk*, I mean actually sit down and have a conversation that doesn't end with your dick inside him."

Beshel would have thrown the man out of his office if he hadn't already left.

What did he know about it? What did he know about anything?

"You know nothing," Beshel shouted at the empty room.

* * * *

After an early dinner with Devin and the kids, Peri helped clean up. With Dasha down for a nap, Devin and Callan settled into the chair in her room and Dev started to read a story to his son. It wasn't long before all three were asleep.

It was a good time to go into the city and check on his own child. There was still plenty of daylight left, and he knew Dr. Thorsel would be there late anyway.

Peri slipped on his shoes and left the house. Peri was acutely aware that Beshel had not been to the Institute. Maybe he was scared. For being so big and tough, he was kind of a baby. Peri and their son were bringing chaos to his ordered life, and Beshel was going to have to deal with it sooner or later.

Sure, he could go by himself, and he would be perfectly fine with that. But he really wanted Beshel to participate. The three of them were going to be stuck together for the rest of their lives. He'd confront him head on if he needed to.

Peri walked around the house into the backyard, and took the path around the lake that led to Beshel's house.

It had been a moderate day. The orange sun still shone bright in the sky. It was a little hot for Peri's liking, but there was a hint of a breeze that made it bearable. The breeze caused ripples across the lake surface, which reflected the purple sky and the wisps of white clouds.

The water was so clear, Peri was tempted to strip naked and jump in. As he neared the back of Beshel's house, scores of wildflowers had grown along the lakeshore. A sweet scent floated across the breeze and Peri inhaled deeply, reveling in the fresh air. Standing amongst the flowers, he dropped to a squat and ran his fingers through the water.

Nice and warm.

It probably stayed like this all year. He would definitely need to come back and take a dip in the water. Standing up, he looked around, taking in the peace and quiet. This would be a lovely place to raise a child. He and Peri could be so happy here, hiding away from the real world and all of its nastiness.

With a sigh, he continued on his walk, ending up at Beshel's front door.

It was the first time he'd been here in the day time. The house was smaller than Bastian's, only one floor, but it was nice. Cozy. It was rustic, appearing as if it was made with wood. The natural stone accents and over-sized windows gave it a decidedly Degan look, though.

Even though Beshel was basically a big government cop, Peri was surprised there wasn't more security—not like there was at Bastian and Devin's home. Peri was able to walk right up to the door and knock.

Beshel opened the door and frowned. "Peri? Is something wrong?"

"No. I just wanted to talk to you."

"Come in."

Following Beshel inside, Peri got a good look at the living room bathed in natural light.

There were a lot of pictures of his family on the walls and on the fireplace mantle, with frames all made of the same wood, all placed with exact precision. There was something… sterile… about the house. If Peri didn't know better, he'd have assumed the pictures were the generic ones that came with the frames.

Perhaps all of the time spent doing his job meant he didn't have time to *live* here, to make it a *home*.

"I was going to go into the city, to visit our baby. Would you like to come with me?"

"I can't. I'm in the middle of work. I have gigs of reading to go through." Beshel held up his comPad. The screen was filled with text.

"Work? Didn't you spend all day at the office?"

"Yes, but I have a lot to do. I am the chief of the bureau and all."

Peri frowned. "Since you're the *chief of the bureau and all*, can't you delegate it to someone else?"

"No." Beshel opened his mouth. "I mean, yes, that is my prerogative. But no."

"Uh, okay… Well, can't you take even a little break?"

"It's a long ride back into the city."

Peri narrowed his eyes. It sounded like he was just making excuses. "And you need to wash your hair after you mop the kitchen floor, right?"

Besh scrunched his brow and tilted his head to the side. "What?"

The puzzled look on his face was almost cute, but Peri was still annoyed with him. "You're avoiding him on purpose."

"I am not."

"You are so."

"I am n—" Beshel sighed. "Look, I can take a little break. Why don't you come in, sit down, and we can talk for a bit."

"Alright."

"Come sit." Beshel sat down and Peri took the space right next to him. He decided to cut Besh a break and changed the subject.

"Oh, you won't believe what Nattie said." Peri let out a nervous laugh. Why the hell did he just say that?

"What?" He covered Peri's hand with his own, squeezing it, urging Peri to continue.

The contact flustered Peri. "She thought we were, uh, screwing. Isn't that funny?"

"And why is that funny?" Beshel moved in closer… close enough to invade Peri's personal space.

"Uh… b-because you don't even like m-me," Peri stammered

in reply. He did not back away, though he knew he should have.

"Who told you that?" Beshel dipped his head, inhaling deeply against the skin of Peri's neck.

"Y-you don't act like it."

"I don't? Then what was that after lunch the other day?"

The warmth of Beshel's lips pressed just under Peri's ear. Peri drew in a sharp breath. They were supposed to be talking, not doing this. "You were horny."

Beshel moved in closer, pressing his body against Peri. His lips ghosted along Peri's jaw until they arrived at his chin. "You were too. There's nothing wrong with two adults enjoying the company of each other."

"Maybe." The word came out in a puff of air that was swallowed by Beshel's mouth just as it came in contact with his.

Screw talking. If this was all he could get, then he'd take it. Someone wanted him, even if it was just for a few minutes. Peri threw his arms around Beshel's neck. He pulled the man down on top of him.

Chapter 12

"Uh-oh. Someone smells!" Peri shook his head, trying desperately to dislodge the foul odor from his brain. "Whew!"

Devin laughed. "You get used to it. Well, kind of. Here, I'll take her." He held out his hands, but Peri pulled the baby closer.

"No, I'll do it. Just show me what to do."

"Okay. You need to learn anyway for when you have your own baby."

Peri stared back at Devin wide-eyed. "What?" How the hell did Devin find out?

"I'm sure someday you're going to have a baby of your own. Come on."

"Right. Yeah. Someday." Peri felt relief that his secret was still safe, but at the same time he felt guilty. He'd never really kept secrets from Devin before, not anything big like this anyway. And this was way beyond *big*. He knew he needed to tell Devin, but he wasn't sure how. He needed to figure things out with Besh first.

Peri followed Devin up to Dasha's bedroom. Devin gave him a complete detailed lesson on how to change a diaper. Callan also watched with great interest. Mishu stood guard at the door, making sure no one else entered the room.

"With boys, you have to be careful they don't let loose a fountain on you."

"A fountain?"

Devin snickered. "You'll see." He looked down at Callan. "This one is notorious."

"What do you do with her tail?" Peri asked.

"You just need to pull it up out of the way." Devin picked up Dasha and laid her against his chest. The soft downy wisps on the tip of her tail stuck out of the back of her diaper. "See?"

"So why do they cut the tails on boys, but not girls?"

"I guess it's a very old tradition." Devin shrugged. "Back when the men used to be feared warriors or something. They cut their tails to keep them from getting in the way during battle."

"That's weird."

"Yeah."

Dasha began to fuss, which turned in a full-blown fit.

Callan's mouth formed an 'O' shape as his eyes widened. "Uh-oh."

Peri agreed with Callan's assessment of the situation.

Devin just laughed. "I think your sister is hungry. Are you hungry too?"

Callan nodded. "Yeah."

While Devin carried Dasha, Callan reached out his hand to Peri. "Unc."

With a smile, Peri took hold of his nephew's hand. He helped him down the stairs, and they all went to the kitchen. Devin pulled the saki milk formula from the fridge and heated it up while Peri put Callan in his booster chair.

Once Devin was feeding Dasha, and Callan had a pile of little star-shaped shortbread cookies, everything quieted down. Devin held Dasha's bottle as he cradled her in his arms. Mishu sat beneath Callan's chair waiting for any cookies the boy might drop down to his best friend.

It was a perfect, calm moment and Peri envied Devin. Not once did Devin panic; he just knew what to do, as if it was instinct. Peri did not have any such instincts. He wondered if maybe Beshel did.

"How did you know Bastian was your bondmate?"

Devin looked up from his daughter's face, keeping the bottle at the right angle without even looking. "Well, I didn't. Bastian knew. Or he should have, I suppose. He didn't know until he... well, until he locked."

Peri frowned. "Locked?"

"Lock," Callan repeated, mouth full of cookie. Wet crumbs splatted to the floor, where Mishu sniffed then licked them up.

Devin chuckled nervously. "Yeah, when we were..." He glanced at Callan and lowered his voice to barely a whisper. "Making love."

Peri's mouth dropped open. "*Locked...*"

"Yeah, *it* swelled. Degan men have these rings..."

Peri knew all about the rings first hand, but he'd never experienced any swelling or locking, thank god. "Oh... It sounds painful."

Devin blushed and looked back down at his baby. "It's not. But it's kind of scary the first time, especially if you're not expecting it. Why do you want to know?"

"I'm having a baby."

The words blurted out of Peri's mouth before his brain could filter them. As soon as they did, he wished he could take them back. Maybe Devin hadn't heard—

Devin gasped in an over-dramatic way. Peri wanted to crawl under a rock.

"You're *pregnant*? Who's the sire? Oh my god, is he your bondmate? Is it someone I know? Is it that scientist you're seeing?" He gasped again. "Is it Uncle Besh? Did you guys *do it* back on Earth? You did! You're not even showing yet, and I was as big as a house. I still *am* as big as a house. That's so not fair. Oh my god, why aren't you saying anything!"

"Devin! Take a breath. Good god. And please don't tell anyone."

A frown pulled across Devin's face. "Why?"

"Because it's complicated."

"I can't promise I won't tell anyone. Especially Bastian."

Peri sighed. "I guess."

"Now tell me what's so complicated about you having a baby."

Callan squealed. "Baby!" He leaned over and dropped a cookie. Mishu caught it mid-air.

Yeah, no way was this going to be a secret for much longer. Peri sank down in his chair. "I don't know where to start…."

"Start from the beginning."

* * * *

"Thank you for seeing me today, Director."

Beshel shook hands with Director Zorn, then sat down in the indicated seat.

Zorn sat back in his chair and steepled his fingers together. "What can I do for you, Chief Drago?"

"I have some questions about Doctor Thorsen."

"Thorsen? Yes, fine."

"How long have you known Doctor Thorsen?"

"I've known him for several years. I met him when I came up the ranks as director. Before that, we didn't have much contact."

"What can you tell me about his research?"

"Much of his research is classified. I would need a court order to discuss that with you."

"Is any of his research weapons related? I see the DSI's weapons budget has increased this past year."

Zorn narrowed his eyes. "We do not conduct research on biological weaponry, if that is what you are implying. Our budget increase is a proper response to the growing threats outside our borders."

"Of course. Does he have contact with outside agencies regarding his research?"

"We don't make a habit of spying on our employees' comings and goings, nor their relationships." He paused. "Though, he did attend a genetics conference about a year ago... I'm sure he must have met and interacted with other geneticists and exobiologists."

"If you could provide me with specific dates, I would appreciate it."

"Naturally. I'll have my assistant send you the data."

* * * *

"Aren't you going to say anything?"

Peri had just spilled his guts to Devin, and his friend still hadn't said a single word. He honestly had no idea how Devin would react.

"Wait here." Devin pushed himself to his feet with a grunt. "Ugh. Even though I've had her, it still feels like I'm pregnant."

Peri chewed on his lip, waiting for Devin. Where had he gone, and why?

"Unc." Callan held out a star cookie.

"Thank you, sweetie." Peri rubbed the top of Callan's head, then took the cookie and nibbled on it. It was bland, but he felt better having something in his stomach.

Devin returned a few minutes later with a tall glass of water. "Here."

Peri took the offered glass, but he was confused. "What—"

"Hold out your hand."

Peri did as requested. Devin dropped a pill into the palm his hand. The pill was the size and color of a raspberry.

"What the heck is this?"

"Birth control. Well, *mutation control* would be more precise."

"Uh, no offense, but this shit don't work, in case you weren't aware of your recent *delicate condition*." Peri pointed at Dasha, asleep in her chair.

"It's a new formula. The doctor says it should work, but I didn't get a chance to try it. Obviously. And there was nothing *delicate* about my condition. I was as big as a freaking house. Hell, I still feel huge."

"You said it, not me."

"Jerk." Devin laughed. "Take your pill."

"Why are you giving this to me?" Peri lifted the pill to his nose and sniffed it. It did *not* smell like a raspberry. "*Ew.* What is this made of?"

"I'm giving it to you because I know you, and I know Degan men. Beshel might try to resist you… But now that he's smelled you… you know, while the two of you—"

"Yeah, yeah, I get it."

"He'll be back, sniffing all over you. Trust me."

"I don't even know if it really happened…"

"Trust me."

With a heavy sigh, Peri popped the pill into his mouth. To say it tasted foul would be an understatement. He washed it down with a healthy gulp of water, nearly choking on it in the process.

"Oh, yeah, I forgot. Your pee might be bright sunshine orange for a couple days."

* * * *

Beshel pinned Peri to the floor. Peri's fists were wrapped around Beshel's shaft. Thick and hard, his cock leaked copious amounts of lubrication. He thrust with abandon, fucking Peri's hands as if they were his ass.

He was going to have that ass next time. Yes, next time, he would bury his cock to the hilt inside Peri. And he wouldn't stop until he shot his load, pumping every single drop inside his little human.

"Peri."

He threw his head back and let out a roar as he erupted. Streams of semen shot out of Beshel's cock, coating Peri's chest and stomach.

Peri let out a series of whimpers as he bucked under Beshel's body.

A sharp pain to the back of his neck shocked Beshel from his dream.

He reached back and rubbed the skin. Was the pain part of the dream, or was it what woke him?

Beshel groaned in disgust as he realized his sleep shorts were wet and sticky. Damn, he hadn't had an actual wet dream since he was a teen. He took a sonic shower to wash off the sweat and semen, but he didn't feel refreshed.

And he still had an erection.

He paced back and forth, his nerves too ramped for sleep. He was never going to get back to sleep. Not like this. If he ever was going to get a decent night's sleep again, he needed to know if these dreams were in actuality memories.

Walking into his office, he turned on the light. He picked up his comPad and called Barlan.

Barlan answered the call, his eyes half-open. He rubbed the sleep away with his fists. "Chief?"

"Sorry to wake you, Barlan. But I need your help."

"Anything, Chief. Just name it."

"I want you to prepare a noötropic memory agent. We might need a neuron stimulator device as well."

"Chief? Those are fairly drastic measures. Do we have a suspect to interrogate?"

"No. It is for me."

Chapter 13

Peri tried to look at Besh, but the Degan refused to look him in the eye. Now that Peri thought about it, Besh seemed awfully nervous. Peri thought he was at Besh's house for a booty call. His pee was neon Tang orange, so he was good to go. Sure, he was slightly embarrassed at how fast he agreed to come over, but now he was embarrassed because he was so obviously wrong about why Besh wanted to see him.

"Is something wrong?" Peri asked.

"Come. Let's sit down."

"Besh?"

"Sit down, Peri. Please."

Peri let Besh lead him to a sofa.

"What's going on? You're freaking me out."

"I know what happened."

"What happened? I'm not following."

"I know *how* it happened. The baby…"

* * * *

Bringing his other hand between their bodies, Peri grabbed the shaft with both hands, using a double-fisting action. He twisted, milking him, making him crazy.

Beshel thrust into Peri's hands with abandon. He'd rather be inside Peri's mouth, or his ass, but he was already too close. He was about to come.

He threw his head back and let out a loud groan. Liquid heat erupted like a geyser from the end of his cock, pulsing in jets over and over, coating Peri's body from the hollow of his neck to the wisps of hair surrounding his groin.

"Besh!"

Peri writhed underneath him. The scent of his semen permeated the air. The scent of *Peri* permeated the air. Beshel inhaled deeply.

A sharp pain in the back of his neck caused Beshel to jerk away from his lover.

From beneath him, Peri gasped and tried to squirm out from under Beshel.

Beshel wanted to reassure him, but his head hurt so fucking bad he couldn't talk. He pulled back, stumbling backward on the floor.

His body felt sluggish as he turned. He reached behind his head and felt something metal. He yanked it free. In his palm, he held a dart. The tailpiece was made of red fibers. The barb end dripped with Beshel's blood. Whatever drug had been inside the needle had been completely injected into him. He needed to call—

"Hit him again."

Who the fuck was that? Beshel turned. The front door was open. Three human men had invaded the apartment, two in military uniforms, and a civilian scientist.

The man in a white lab coat clutched a medical case to his chest. He had red hair, greying at the temples. Behind a pair of spectacles, his eyes were wide, and his face was drained of color. "Hit him again!" he repeated, his voice high-pitched in panic.

Both soldiers raised their guns.

Another dart hit Beshel square in the chest. The other hit Peri, who slumped to the ground with a whimper.

Beshel tried to scream, but nothing came out. His vision blurred as he crawled toward an unconscious Peri. He reached Peri, covering and protecting him, just before his body went limp. The room went dark. He could still make out shapes and could hear their voices, though it sounded like they were underwater.

Beshel felt his body being pushed away from Peri. He wanted to resist the intruders, to protect his human, but he couldn't move. His muscles were locked.

"This is even better," the high-pitched ginger man said. "I'd hoped to collect some of Devin McSmith's DNA... but we've got fresh semen and live gametes."

Another voice made a throaty sound. "Don't really need the commentary. Just hurry the fuck up, Doc."

"I don't know if they will produce the same results as the first batch, though..." The shadow of the smaller man crouched over Peri's limp body.

"That's fucking nasty, Doc."

"Okay, I've got it all. Maybe we should take the Degan with us... If this works, we could harvest his seed. Oh! He's still conscious. Give him another dose, aim for the brainstem."

Beshel was rolled onto his stomach. Agony flared at the base of his skull.

Everything went black.

* * * *

Peri stared at Besh with a look of horror on his face.

"They took me with them, but I woke up before they could get me in the hovercar. Their tranquilizers weren't properly calibrated for a humanoid my size."

"I don't understand."

"I somehow made it back to the hotel and passed out. When I woke that next day, I didn't remember anything that happened the night before. It's a side effect of the tranqs they used. Honestly, I don't think they expected us to be in the apartment. I think they were there to collect any DNA samples they could of Devin and Bastian."

"But instead they caught us... you know... on the floor."

"Yes."

"And they used it to..."

"Yes."

"I think I'm gonna be sick."

Peri shot up from the sofa and raced into the bathroom.

* * * *

"I'm sorry."

Peri looked at Devin, confused. He'd just told Devin how his baby had been created. "What? Why are you sorry?"

Devin hung his head. "If they hadn't come to search my stuff, then they never would've…"

"Hey." Peri scooted closer to Devin. "Stop. It's not your fault."

Bastian walked into the room, carrying a freshly bathed Dasha, with a damp-haired Callan trailing behind him. The boy's wet hair lay flat against his head, accentuating the small horns on his head. His eyes were drooping. Naturally, Mishu was in tow behind the boy.

Peri bit his lip as he watched Bastian. "Did you hear any of that?"

"I heard some." He gave Dasha to Devin, then pressed a kiss on top of Devin's head. "I'll get her bottle."

Peri tickled Dasha's tiny little toes. "You make such pretty babies, Dev. So cute."

"Da." Callan gripped the edge of the sofa cushion and bounced on his feet, looking at Devin expectedly. Since Dev had his hands full, Peri lifted the boy, setting him between Devin and himself. Callan leaned his head against his daddy. He rubbed his eyes with his fist. Within seconds, he was asleep.

"I'm sure your baby boy will be just as cute," Devin said. "Have you thought of what you wanted to name him yet?"

"No. Not really." Peri let out a short puff of air. "God, if I did that, then it would be *real*. To be honest, I haven't really thought about anything. I have no idea what we're going to do, where we're going to go…."

"*Go?* What are you talking about? You're not going anywhere, Per. You're staying here with us."

Peri shook his head. "I can't do that. You've got your own family. We'd just be in the way."

"What are you talking about? You *are* family, Peri. You don't

84

have to do this alone."

Bastian returned with a bottle, and he gave it to Devin. "Martan called. He's home on leave. He's dying to meet his new niece." He placed a hand on Peri's shoulder. "You are as much a brother to me as Martan. You and your son will always be welcome in our home. Always."

Peri nodded and smiled. He heard the words from Bastian and Devin, but he also knew it wouldn't take long before he wore out his welcome.

Chapter 14

Beshel had just taken a bite of his sandwich when his comPad chimed. He glanced down at the screen and saw that Corporal Durant was calling him. He hadn't spoken to the human Marine since they'd left Centauri Colony and went their separate ways. He'd call him back after he finished lunch. Right now he wasn't in the mood for conversation.

He hadn't spoken to Peri since he'd told him what had happened back on Earth. That was three days ago. It had shaken Peri to finally discover the truth, to know how the embryo had been created. Beshel knew exactly how he felt, though.

He also wondered what would have happened if they hadn't shown up. Would things have progressed further between them? Did the scientist intervening also stop what might have grown into a real relationship?

It didn't matter, though. It was done. Instead of building a family, he had a child grown in a lab, and a supremely fucked up relationship with—

"How dare you!"

Beshel jerked at the sound of his brother's voice. When did Dashel get so damn sneaky? Or was Beshel losing his touch?

Why couldn't he enjoy his lunch in peace? It was a beautiful day out and there was a gentle breeze floating through the Capital square. Beshel just wanted to take a break from work and eat a quiet meal.

With a sigh, Beshel set down his sandwich. "What am I daring about now, Dash?"

Dashel sat down at Beshel's table. His face already stern, red with anger, he leaned forward, and thankfully lowered his voice to an acceptable volume. "Why am I finding out about this second-hand?"

"Finding out what?"

Dashel slammed his hands on the table and shot him a disdainful stare. "You know damn well what. Peri? The child?"

Someone had a big mouth, and whoever it was needed to be punished. "Because it's none of your damn business. Just because you're governor of this province, it doesn't give you the right to butt into everyone's lives."

"I more than have the right. That child is part of the family. Is Peri your bondmate?"

Beshel dismissed Dashel's words with a scoff and a wave of his hand. "That's nonsense."

"Don't you dare diminish what I have with Nydia with a wave of your hand."

"I didn't say anything about you, did I? But if you want to believe that trite drivel, then go right ahead. Some of us live in a more enlightened age."

"We have had this argument more than once, Besh, and I won't have it again. Nydia is my true bondmate. You have closed yourself off so completely, that if you can't see it, investigate it, touch it, then it isn't real. Well, let me tell you something. Just because you can't hold it in your hand, that doesn't mean it's not real."

"I'm not interested in rehashing this old argument with you. Let me finish my lunch in peace."

"Can you honestly tell me you don't feel something for Peri?"

"That's not what I said. Just because I don't believe in so-called 'true bondmates' doesn't mean I'm an emotionless automaton."

"You could have fooled me. Peri is frightened and alone. He is going to raise *your* child. Your *son*, Besh. He has this notion in his head that he will be raising the baby by himself. If you aren't going to grow up and do your duty, then I will. And there will be consequences."

Dashel's holier-than-thou attitude was really rubbing Beshel the wrong way. "And what does that mean?"

"I will take that boy in, and Nydia and I will help to raise his son. That child will want for nothing. And you— You will no longer be welcome in our home. You will be dead to our family."

"You wouldn't dare."

"Watch me."

Beshel slammed his fists on the table and rose to his feet. "Who do you think you are? Peri is mine! He and the child are *my* responsibility. If you don't back off, I will—"

A rumbling in the distance interrupted Beshel's tirade. The ground beneath him trembled. A flock of birds flew overhead, screeching as they fled from danger. Around the square people had stopped and there was even a startled scream in the distance.

Beshel couldn't remember the last time he'd felt a quake on the homeworld. This region of their planet was geologically stable—

The unmistakable sound of an explosion grabbed Beshel's attention. He turned toward the source. In the distance, he could see the three towers of the Degan Science Institute.

A section of the smaller tower was engulfed in flames. Fire and black smoke poured from it. A second explosion rocked the building, and many of the windows of the middle tower exploded outwards, shooting shards of glass to the ground below.

"My gods," Dashel whispered from somewhere behind.

Beshel gasped in horror as the realization hit him.

Chapter 15

Beshel raced as fast as he could to the Institute. He had the hovercar's sirens on and he dodged traffic, until it came to a complete stop. Traffic in and out of the institute was at a total standstill. He slammed his fist on the horn, but it was useless.

"Fuck!"

Abandoning his car, he ran the rest of the way on foot.

Dashel had gone back to his office to coordinate with the provincial government. They promised to keep in touch, to share any information they could with each other.

Beshel didn't know if it was a terrorist attack, or if maybe it was an industrial accident. What he did know was that he had a job to do. He pulled out his comPad as he pushed his way through the crowd, and connected to Agent Barlan.

"Barlan."

"Chief." Barlan was out of breath.

"Get as many men as you can to the Science Institute."

"We're already on the way, every agent I could pull from the office. I'm on foot, but I should be there in a few minutes."

"Find me when you get here." Beshel disconnected the comm.

When he arrived at the towers, it was utter chaos. A crowd of spectators was already gathering on the grounds as the three buildings were being evacuated. There were scientists and civilians everywhere. Fire crews struggled to contain the damage. Paramedics were starting to arrive to help the injured.

A security guard stopped Beshel before he could get close to the building. "Sorry, but I need you to turn around and move away from the building."

Beshel pulled his credentials from his vest pocket. "Federation Chief Investigator Beshel Drago."

"Go right in, sir. They're setting up a base of operations to the left." He pointed toward the lobby.

"Thank you. And get these people back. They need to be on the other side of the street at a minimum. Gather your men. Do it now."

Beshel hung the badge around his neck, and pushed his way through the crowds that were fleeing the buildings. The fire crews had their act together and were already working to extinguish the flames. But with all the people stumbling around, the paramedics were having difficulty getting to their patients.

When he found the "base of operations", he was appalled. One of the Institute's security guards had taken charge. Holding a communicator to his mouth, he was flustered and out of his depth as he stared helplessly at the chaos around him. The Institute clearly didn't have enough emergency disaster training to deal with a situation like this. Beshel didn't have time to deal with the guard.

"Chief Investigator Drago. I'm taking over. Give me your report."

"Uh…"

"Hey!" Beshel called out to a paramedic crew. "Set up triage over here, away from the fire crew."

"Yes, sir."

Agent Barlan appeared with a handful of agents, ready to work. "Where do you want us, Chief?"

"Coordinate with the police, fire crew, paramedics. Make sure the civilians are cleared, and maintain a safe distance. We need to start questioning the guards and employees. Find out if anyone saw anything. I want this to go smoothly. As soon as the fire crew clears the building, I want to lead a team inside."

"On it, Chief."

A familiar face caught Beshel's eye. Director Zorn stumbled from the building lobby. He looked to be in pretty bad shape. His clothes were torn and covered with soot. Blood poured down the side of his head. Beshel jogged over and took the Director's side, helping him stand upright.

"I got wounded over here," Beshel called out to the paramedics as he steered the man to the triage area. Barlan ran up and took the man's other side.

A nurse tended to the deep cut on the man's forehead, cleaning the wound and dressing it.

"Director, can you tell us what happened?"

He cleared his throat. His voice came out tight and strained. "It was the exobiology lab."

Beshel wanted to vomit. He balled his hands into fists to keep them from shaking. It wasn't as if he didn't already know, but to hear it voiced out loud... *Pull yourself together.* He had a job to do; he couldn't think about anything else right now.

"What about Dr. Thorsel?"

Zorn shook his head. "He didn't make it." He closed his eyes and drew in a breath. When he exhaled, it came out in a stutter. "His leg was injured. He was too slow. I had to close the bulkhead. If I hadn't, we would have lost the entire floor."

He began to cough, a deep hacking that produced a thick black soot. It coated his hand and his chin. The nurse gave him a towel and a bottle of water. He downed half of the bottle in one gulp before he started coughing again.

"I saw them," Zorn added, his voice nearly gone. He wiped his mouth with the back of his hand.

"Saw who?" Beshel pressed.

"Humans," he spat. "They came for the incubator... took it."

Beshel traded a look with Barlan.

Zorn coughed. "Union. They wore... Union uniforms."

Chapter 16

Beshel sighed as he looked down the corridor. He rubbed the back of his neck as he took in the damage. The blast doors, closed by Director Zorn, had stopped the explosion from taking out the rest of the floor, but on the other side of the doors was nothing but destruction.

They didn't have a lot of time to examine the lab. The fire chief was concerned there could be structural damage to the subfloor. Seeing the damage firsthand, he agreed the chief was right to be concerned.

"Fuck."

Agent Barlan sighed from behind him. "You've been hanging around the humans too long; you've picked up their curses. But *fuck* is a damned good word to describe this."

"Yeah." Beshel pulled on a pair of sterile gloves.

He rubbed a finger across the wall and examined the black soot left on his glove. Whatever they'd used to set off the explosion demolished the hallway. It burned hot enough to begin to melt the metal columns. Everything in sight was charred black, reeking of burnt plastics and electronics. A scorched metallic scent hung in the air so thick Beshel could taste it, and it was *not* pleasant.

Water and foam from the fire crew's suppressants covered everything, leaving oily and frothy puddles on the floor.

Just inside the blast doors lay a smoldering corpse. Though little more than a blackened skeleton, Beshel knew without scanning it was Dr. Thorsel. The man had died not more than a foot away from safety.

"Catalog him, the poor bastard..."

Beshel carefully stepped over the corpse, moving further into the hallway. Barlan and two other agents followed. The three of them used comPads to scan and document every square centimeter of the site.

Beshel reached the hole that should have been the door to Thorsel's lab. Stepping around the rubble as best as he could, he made his way to the back corner. The incubator did not appear to be among the ruined equipment.

They had taken his son. His helpless, defenseless son.

Beshel picked up a melted hunk of metal and threw it across the room.

"Fuck!" Agent Barlan shouted as he side-stepped the projectile. "Chief? You okay?" Barlan looked around the room and shook his head in disbelief.

Beshel reeled in his rage. He would save it for when he found the men who did this. He would make them pay. "Did you get the security footage?"

"No. The cameras conveniently went offline just before they entered. How did they get into the building without alerting security? Surely the lobby guards would have seen a unit of Union soldiers— humans—and triggered an alarm."

"They had help."

"Chief," one of the agents called out. "Over here."

Beshel and Barlan made their way to the other side of the lab.

"It looks like the doctor might've got one of them," he said.

The agent stood over a scorched body. The body was smaller in size, and the skull had no cranial horns. Its ears were in the wrong spot, and the upper and lower teeth were all smooth. The corpse was not Degan.

Barlan looked up from his pad and voiced what Beshel already knew.

"He's human."

* * * *

Peri and Devin were glued to the vid screen in Bastian's office. While Bastian spoke with his father via comPad, the two humans watched the news report. Bastian's younger brother Martan was on leave and he'd come over for a visit when the news broke out.

Terrorists had attacked the Degan Science Institute in the Capital City. The total death count was still unknown, but there were numerous injuries. It was unconfirmed, but the rumors were that the terrorists were humans.

Peri wanted to burst into tears. "I should be there."

"It's not safe, Per."

"They took him, Dev. Those scientists. I just know it."

A visible shudder travelled through Devin's body. "You don't know that."

He couldn't even look Peri in the eyes when he said it. But Peri knew it was true. And Devin knew it as well. The men who had done this, they'd taken his baby. To them, he was nothing more than a bunch of cells to harvest… to make weapons and who knows what other horrendous uses they came up with.

"Uncle Besh is on the scene," Martan said. "He'll get to the bottom of what's going on."

Peri and Devin traded looks. Of course Beshel was on the scene, but now Peri was worried about *him* too.

"I'm a little worried about Mother," Martan admitted. "But I suppose the Prime Minister's building is the safest place to be right now."

"Mother is fine, brother." Bastian had ended his conversation. "So is Sire."

"Did you find out anything?" Peri asked. He didn't want to be rude and interrupt, but his world was falling apart.

Bastian glanced over at Devin. He sighed softly. "Their target was the exobiology lab… I'm so sorry, Peri, but they stole the incubator."

Peri's stomach dropped, then threatened to empty itself of his lunch. His baby boy had been taken. He couldn't defend himself. He couldn't even survive on his own. He needed Peri.

Cradling Dasha against his chest, Devin gulped. "Do they know who?"

"Besh said witnesses are saying it was humans. In Union uniforms."

Devin buried his face in his daughter's blanket. "Oh god... It's them."

Peri jumped to his feet. "We have to go after them!"

Lifting his head, Devin shot Peri a worried frown. "I don't think that's a good idea, Peri. These people are dangerous. I'm sure Uncle Besh and his team are right on their trail."

"I'm not going to sit around. It's not your baby, Dev. He's *mine*. Don't tell me you wouldn't go after Callan if they took him. You know what they'll do to him."

Devin's eyes brimmed with unshed tears. He looked down at his son, playing on the floor with the banti. "You're right, Per. I would." He looked back at his husband. "Bastian, I need you to—"

Peri shook his head. "No. He has to stay here. You need him. Your family needs him."

"But, Per, you can't do it alone. You need someone who can pilot a ship, who can track—"

"I'll help you."

Peri turned toward Martan. "What?"

"I said I'd help you."

* * * *

"Out of the way!"

Beshel pushed through the angry crowd gathered at the Prime Minister's building in the Capitol Square.

The damned xenophobes were like vultures. The news of the attack had barely hit the airwaves before they showed up in the Square to protest. It was like they already knew to be here, and they showed up in bigger numbers, too. Marching back and forth, they screamed anti-alien epithets. They held signs calling for the expulsion of all off-worlders from the Federation borders.

If that wasn't bad enough, news outlets were gathering. It wouldn't be long before their protest hit the news channels. Normally, these lunatics wouldn't be taken seriously, but this latest incident was exactly what they needed to build momentum for their cause.

Beshel met Dashel in front of the building. His older brother looked worried, and Beshel didn't blame him. Inside the building, security had been stepped up. The number of Degan Armed Forces soldiers normally stationed in the building had doubled.

Dashel reached out and clasped Beshel's shoulder. "It's good to see you safe."

"You too, Dash."

"I've already been in touch with my children, urging them to stay home. It is especially important for Devin, Peri, and the children."

Beshel did not miss the way Dashel included Peri. He took one last look at the angry protesters. There was no telling what they'd do if they ran into any humans now. "Agreed."

"I'm trying to get the police department to take care of the protestors. Ignorant bigots." Dashel sneered. "Come. The Prime Minister is waiting."

Beshel followed Dashel up the stairs to the second floor. They were only allowed to proceed after showing their credentials and being patted down.

Nydia stood outside the Prime Minister's office. Her brow was furrowed and her tail twitched, swinging in a nervous manner. When she saw Dashel, she relaxed noticeably. The two embraced tightly. Dashel rubbed his cheek against hers, then pressed a tender kiss to her lips.

"Ready?" Dashel asked softly.

She nodded and the three of them entered the prime minister's office. The room was crowded with high ranking military personnel and other advisors. Dashel wasn't the only provincial governor present. Beshel counted three others.

Director Zorn was present, his head wrapped in a bandage, and his left arm bound in a sling. Beshel didn't think his injuries were that severe. He spoke quietly with the Prime Minister.

Prime Minister Arden was an older man, the hair on his head gone almost entirely grey. While normally jovial, today he was visibly agitated as he talked to Zorn.

When he saw Beshel, he nodded his chin. "Let's get started."

There weren't enough seats for everyone at the conference table, but Beshel made sure Nydia was seated before joining her. Dashel stood behind her chair.

Once everyone had settled, Arden got right down to it. "Ambassador Drago, have you spoken with Union HQ?" he asked Nydia.

She nodded respectfully. "I have been on comm with Union President Sylenas for the past hour. The Union had nothing to do with this attack."

"That may be so, but it *was* humans." He turned to Beshel. "Chief, what has your department found?"

"We recovered the remains of a human at the attack site. Eyewitness reports say they wore Union uniforms. However, I don't feel we should jump to—"

Arden cut him off with a wave of his hand. "This is not the first time we have run into problems with these humans."

"I was there," Zorn interjected. "These weren't just humans. They were Union soldiers."

Arden nodded along with Zorn's words. "And I am not convinced the Union did not know of their activities. Therefore, I have no other choice. I am closing our borders to the Galactic Planetary Union."

The room was completely silent. The Degans had not gone to war in over a century, and even then, it was just a minor border skirmish with the Mirans.

Dashel shifted his weight between his feet. He swallowed so loudly Beshel could hear it from where he was sitting. "Begging your pardon, sir. What of the off-worlders here who may belong to Union species? My province especially has a high percentage of non-Degan citizens."

"I am not unsympathetic to your situation, Governor, both professionally and *personally*. Any non-Degan off-worlders living as citizens inside our borders—human included—can stay if they desire. Any Union military or civilian personnel must leave immediately." He glanced at Nydia. "Let your embassy know it has one day to evacuate. If any Union troops or vessels cross the Federation's borders, it will be considered an act of war." He turned to the men sitting to his right.

"General. Admiral. Prepare your troops."

Chapter 17

Peri packed a quick bag and met Martan by the front door. "I'm ready."

"I just got off the comm with Uncle Beshel," Bastian said. "He and my parents are on their way here. He said it was important we stay in the house. It's not safe for you out there."

"I won't sit around and do nothing. The longer we wait, the further away they're getting."

"They should be here in a few minutes. We'll decide what to do then."

"I'll go by myself if I have to. I'll hire a ship."

Bastian looked sympathetic. "Peri, you don't understand. The Degan Federation has closed its borders. We're preparing to go to war with the Union. They're calling for the expulsion of all off-worlders."

Devin gasped. He held Dasha tighter, and hurried over to Callan. With a hand on the boy's shoulder, he held him against his legs. "They can't make us leave, can they? Aren't our children citizens of the Degan Federation?"

Quickly crossing the distance, Bastian picked up Callan and put his arm around Devin. "You became a citizen when we bonded. This is our home. No one is making us go anywhere, my true one. I promise."

The outer gate chimed, and Martan activated the panel by the front door. "They're here." He tapped a button to open the gate.

A few minutes later, they were all sitting in Bastian's office. Peri stood by the door, impatient, ready to leave. No one here understood. It wasn't their baby who had been stolen. They didn't care.

Dashel had turned on the wall vid screen. News reports of the attack and the demonstrations played non-stop.

Devin sat on the couch with Bastian and his children. He was visibly shaken: trembling, on the verge of tears.

"You're not being forced to leave," Dashel explained. "But as you can see, it's not safe for you."

Peri was sick of hearing that. "If we track these people down, we can prove the Union wasn't involved. Maybe the Prime Minister will call off the war."

Beshel looked up from his pad. "That's what I'm working on."

"Well, let's go then!" Peri snapped.

After tucking his pad into his pocket, Beshel took Peri aside, leading him into the living room. He placed his hands on Peri's shoulders. "I would prefer it if you stayed here, with Bastian's family."

Peri shook his head. "You have no say over what I do or don't do."

"Peri—"

"No. That's the way you wanted it. Remember?"

Beshel reached out and cupped Peri's chin. He leaned down and when Peri met his eyes, he spoke softly. "I want you to be safe. Do you not understand that?"

The tenderness in Beshel's expression shocked Peri. It was the first time Besh had shown him genuine affection, or any kind of emotion beyond lust or impatience. To cement it, Besh bent in closer and pressed a soft kiss to Peri's lips.

Peri pushed up on his tip-toes and returned the kiss, letting Besh know that he returned the sentiment.

"I want you to be safe, too."

"You *have* to be safe," Beshel whispered.

"Then take me with you."

Beshel chuckled mirthlessly. "You are so stubborn."

Peri smiled. "Just like you."

* * * *

Beshel, Peri and Martan met Agent Barlan at the space dock.

The plan was for Martan to get clearance to leave the planet to rendezvous with his unit on Degan Station. Beshel and Peri would tag along for the ride without anyone knowing.

Dressed in a full-length robe, Peri kept the hood up over his head to hide the fact he was human. Of course, his size made him stand out as much as the silly "disguise."

"Are you sure this is a good idea?" Barlan asked. "Our entire department is being recalled home. They are going to notice when the bureau chief comes up missing."

"I'm damn positive it's a bad idea, but I have to do this. Do you have the data on their escape vessel?"

"Yes. I pulled it directly off the satellite. It's already loaded to your comPad. I'll try to keep the Prime Minister off your back."

Beshel clasped Barlan's shoulder. "Thanks, Barlan."

"Good hunting, Chief."

Once the shuttle cleared the planet, they went off course, passing Degan Station on their way out of the solar system.

Beshel was studying the data provided by Barlan on his comPad when an incoming call interrupted him. It was Marine Corporal Durant again. Beshel answered the call and the gruff soldier's face appeared on his screen.

"Corporal, what can I do for you?"

"For starters, tell me what in the holy hell is going on. We got a lead on the suspected muscle hired by the scientists, a band of mercs. The *Artemis* was en route to intercept. When we realized they were heading for the Degan system, I tried to contact you."

Beshel wanted to kick himself. "Fuck." If he'd taken Durant's call earlier, he probably wouldn't have been able to stop the attack, but he might have been able to stop them before they escaped. "They hit the Science Institute dressed as Union soldiers, and stole the incubator carrying the fetus. Where are you now?"

"About ten light years away from Alpha Ursae Majoris."

"Whatever you do, *do not* cross into our space. I repeat, do not cross into our space, or you'll be the ones who triggered the start of an interstellar war."

"Union HQ has given us an all stop order. We're sitting here with our thumbs up our asses waiting for further orders."

"We should rendezvous and pool our resources."

"Agreed."

Martan brought up a star chart. He pointed to one of the star systems. "We could meet here, in the Narenda system."

After a moment, Durant nodded. "Captain Bragman has agreed. See you in a few hours. Durant out."

While Martan changed course, Beshel swiveled in his chair to check on Peri.

Peri stared out the shuttle's viewport. Still wearing the robe, he looked so small. He had this forlorn look on his face, and Beshel felt compelled to try to fix it.

Beshel unbuckled his seat straps and moved to the back. He squatted in front of Peri's chair, and pushed the hood back, exposing Peri's beautiful face. "Are you okay?" he asked.

Peri didn't say anything. He just shook his head, never taking his teary eyes off whatever they were focused on out the window.

"Are we gonna find him, Besh? Our—" His voice cracked and he stopped mid-sentence. He drew in a stilted breath.

Seeing Peri so emotional affected Beshel in a way he never expected.

"We'll find him, Peri. I promise you."

Peri shook his head again. "You can't make promises like that."

Beshel reached out and used his fingers to turn Peri's head and lift his chin. "I can, and I pledge to you I will find our child, and I will bring him home."

* * * *

"Degan Shuttle 84656, you are cleared for landing in Bay 2. U.S.C.

Artemis *out.*"

Martan guided the shuttle toward the *Artemis*'s docking bay doors. Though not as formidable as a Degan X-class battleship, the Union Navy *Epsilon*-class cruiser was still a respectable size.

Once the shuttle had docked and the bay had pressurized, Beshel hit the airlock control. He walked down the ramp, followed by Peri and Martan.

Beshel immediately recognized Corporal Durant. Standing with the Marine were a human and a Sargan.

The Sargan wore the uniform of a Union Navy captain, and was clearly the ship's commanding officer, Captain Bragman. Typical of males of his species, he had pale blue skin and silver eyes. His characteristic gray-white hair was cut in a short spiky style common with Union military.

The human was small in stature with black hair, and his uniform bore the markings of someone in the science division. He was nicely built for a small man. His skin was a shade darker than Peri's, and his eyes were almond-shaped.

Durant stepped forward and shook Beshel's hand. "Chief. Welcome." He introduced the men at his side. "This is Captain Bragman and Lieutenant Kanataka, ship's head science officer. Chief Investigator Beshel Drago."

Beshel recognized the lieutenant's name from the *Cassini* mission logs. He'd helped Aron Adler rescue the frozen embryo from XP-8460. "Lieutenant, it's good to meet you."

Beshel shook each man's hand, then motioned toward his companions. "This is Peri McSmith and Lieutenant Martan Drago."

Peri waved his hand while Martan dipped his chin respectfully.

"You two related?" Durant asked.

"Martan is my nephew."

Durant's eyes cut to Peri. Beshel knew he was curious, but frankly who Peri was to Beshel was no one's business.

"Welcome aboard the U.S.C. *Artemis*," Bragman greeted the three visitors.

"Thank you, Captain. It is vital we recover the stolen cargo. If we can capture these rogues, then maybe we can stop a war at the same time."

"Of course, Chief Drago. I understand perfectly what's at stake here. We've re-programmed our sensors in an attempt to track the rogue vessel, but I understand you have close range data?"

"Yes. Lieutenant Drago can provide our satellite data."

"Excellent. Please work with Lieutenant Kanataka."

The human lieutenant smiled. "If you care to follow me to the science lab, we can program the sensors. I've also been in touch with Dr. Aron Adler, and I have all the necessary equipment set up and ready for the baby's recovery, if you'd like to inspect it."

Martan held out his hand toward the door. "Lead the way, Lieutenant Kanataka."

"You can call me Kenji."

The corner of Martan's mouth turned up ever so slightly. "Kenji. Call me Martan."

From behind him, Beshel heard Peri sigh.

Chapter 18

Peri looked around the room and frowned. He shrugged off his robe and tossed it on a chair, then put his hands on his hips. "Are we supposed to share quarters? Why would they assume we're sharing?"

"Perhaps space is limited."

"Perhaps you and Martan should share then." Peri looked out the viewport, and his eyes began to droop. Shaking it off, he looked around their assigned quarters. Like his room on the *Cassini*, the window spanned nearly the entirety of one wall. Set at the front of the ship, their assigned room was generous in size, and located in the perfect spot. "You can move in with him. I want this room."

"When was the last time you got a decent night's sleep?" Beshel asked.

Peri shrugged.

"Come here. I'd like you to get some rest."

Beshel pulled Peri toward the bed and began unbuttoning his shirt.

"How am I supposed to rest when our baby has been kidnapped?" Peri's voice sounded whiny, but he couldn't help it. And he was too tired to stop Beshel from stripping off his clothes.

"There is nothing to be done, not by me or by you. Not until we track the ship, and then we will recover the fetus. Did I not promise you?"

"Don't call it that. It's a baby. *Our* baby boy."

Beshel paused for a moment. "I apologize."

"Don't apologize, Besh." Peri sighed. "Just *feel*. We're having a baby, Besh. Don't you feel anything?"

"Of course I do. I feel *you*." Beshel's warm hands ran down the sides of Peri's body.

Peri's eyes fluttered shut as his body reacted to the touch of his lover.

"Promise me you'll stay safe," Beshel whispered. "I couldn't bear to lose you, too."

Beshel dropped to his knees and began to mouth Peri's dick through this pants. He could feel the warmth of Besh's mouth even through the material. Blood pumped south and his dick rapidly began to fill.

With a yank of his snap and a tug of the zipper, Besh freed Peri from the confines of his pants. He engulfed Peri's hard dick into his hot mouth. Wet heat and a silky slick tongue coupled with a gentle sucking motion pulled an unabashed moan from Peri's lips. Peri almost crumpled to the floor.

None of his lovers before Besh had been so concerned with his pleasure. And Besh was so good at giving it.

"I'm on the pill," Peri whispered.

"The what?"

"Devin gave me an anti-mutation pill. We can make love without worrying…"

"Yes." Beshel let out an animalistic growl. "I want to *feel you*."

He practically ripped Peri's clothes off before stripping himself. Peri took the opportunity to watch Beshel undress, and to get a good look at the man. His entire body was covered with fur, a pretty shade of amber. It was darker and thicker on his chest and stomach. He was quite broad across the shoulders and back, surprisingly narrow at the waist—like an exaggerated child's action figure. Only Besh's body wasn't a toy, especially what he carried between his legs.

Good god, his cock was huge. It was pointed directly at Peri like a heat seeking missile, and he realized he'd just committed to taking that inside his body.

"Besh… I've never…"

Beshel's eyebrows knitted together. "Never?"

Now Peri felt like a freak. "I was waiting for the right guy, and I never seem to get past a first or second date. It's stupid—"

"No. It's not stupid. That you want to give yourself to me… It means more to me than you know. And I will be gentle. I promise."

"I know you will."

Peri climbed onto the bed and rolled over onto his belly. He was already developing feelings for Besh, whether he wanted to admit it or not. If they were face-to-face when Beshel took his virginity, he'd probably never recover from the inevitable heartbreak. Besh would eventually leave him, just as everyone else had.

"Oh!"

The pitiful thoughts were immediately replaced when he felt the slippery heat of Beshel's tongue swipe through the crack of his ass.

"Oh god…" Peri squeezed his eyes shut and gripped the bed covers in his fists.

Beshel had pulled apart his cheeks with his rough hands and was now going to town on him.

Peri lost track of time as Beshel prepared him to take the beastly monstrosity between his legs. His tongue and fingers stretched him and relaxed him. Those knowing fingers massaged his insides, knowing exactly where to touch him. While his fingers worked him, Beshel lapped at his balls.

He was dripping onto the sheets below him, on the verge of coming all over the place. Pushing his ass back against Beshel's fingers, he pleaded. "Please, Besh. I need you now." God, even the smallest of movements shot waves of pleasure through his cock as it rubbed against the sheets. He was so close, but he wanted Besh to be inside him when it happened. "Please."

Peri thought he was ready, but he wasn't. The head of Beshel's cock was hot like a potato fresh from the oven, slippery with the copious fluid that was continuously leaking from the slit. When it pressed against Peri's opening and breached it, Peri felt like he'd been punched in the gut.

The shock pulled him back from the edge of orgasm and his dick started to soften. Gritting his teeth, he fisted the blankets. Beshel's massive body rested lightly on top of him, keeping the bulk of his weight free. Whispered words of encouragement and kisses along Peri's shoulders and the back of his head didn't do much to alleviate the pain.

"Relax, Peri," Beshel purred into his ear.

Peri's eyes fluttered closed as Besh's lips tickled that spot below his ear in just the right way. *Oh, yes.* Peri wanted this. He wanted to share this with Besh, the sire of his baby.

After another moment the pain started to dissipate. There was still discomfort, but it no longer felt like Beshel was splitting him in half.

"That's it… There you go."

Beshel's body shifted, sending another inch into him. He began to move, ever so slowly, gradually going deeper and deeper. When Beshel hit that spot inside him, Peri felt his body respond. His dick hardened again, and he realized he was moaning.

The fur on Beshel's torso tickled his back and ass as Beshel rested more of his weight on Peri. The rhythm of his hips picked up speed, sending his cock deep into Peri's body. The Degan's panting breath was hot against his ear.

An overwhelming scent engulfed Peri, making him lightheaded. "Oh, wow… What is—"

One of Beshel's hands slid underneath Peri and engulfed his shaft.

Peri was now moaning with abandon, thrusting his cock into the grip of Besh's slick fist, then pushing back to meet his relentless cock.

"Yes, Besh!"

"Peri," Beshel groaned into his ear. It sent a shudder down Peri's entire body. "You feel so good. You're mine now. I'm never letting you go."

It was all too much. Besh's words, the touch of his hand, the ramming of his cock, the heat of his breath and the kisses on his ear and neck. And that wonderful smell.

Peri opened his mouth to scream Besh's name, but his breath

stopped.

He exploded, filling Besh's fist and the sheets below him.

* * * *

Beshel felt the tension in his groin building. Peri was coming undone beneath him, and his ass was clamping down around his cock. The smell of Peri's semen and the sounds of his orgasm threw Beshel to the edge.

He needed to pull out, or he'd put Peri at risk, knowing those medications were experimental and unproven. He felt lightheaded for a split-second as his cock throbbed.

It throbbed again, and Besh could actually feel his cock swell in size.

Peri moaned. "Oh god, you're so big!"

The pleasure was almost too much as all of the blood in his body seemingly rushed to his groin.

Peri was so fucking tight. Beshel felt an almost uncontrollable urge to shove his cock into Peri's heat as far as he could and hold it. When he felt another wave coming on, urging him to thrust forward. In a panic, he pulled his cock free.

He looked down at his cock. The rings along the shaft of his erection swelled and throbbed as his groin muscles contracted. They did it again, only this time the rings swelled up and stayed that way, making his cock nearly twice as thick as normal. He didn't have time to think about how that had never happened to him before.

His internal muscles contracted so hard it felt like a punch to the nuts. It was followed by a feeling of pure euphoria as they released.

"Peri!" he cried as his cock leapt, sending a stream of semen splattering across Peri's back. Over and over, he released, until he had coated Peri's back and ass with cum.

"Oh god," Peri softly moaned. "Besh... It's so warm, so hot..."

Beshel had never released such a vast amount of cum in his life. It was all over the place, all over Peri, even in his hair. Something was different this time.

He stared down at his monstrous erection, engorged and purple, clear fluid still dripping from the slit, to spill down the shaft. Looking at the swollen rings, he realized if he'd been inside Peri when he came, he would have been stuck. He would have locked. And that meant...

Peri lifted his head and looked back at Beshel, his eyelids droopy. "Is everything okay?"

Beshel tore his eyes from his cock to look at Peri. "Yes. Everything is fine."

Before Peri could see what had happened, Beshel got up and found Peri's underwear. He used it to wipe Peri's backside clean. It wasn't enough fabric for the job. He picked up the T-shirt and cleaned the rest of him.

Peri softly sighed. "That's nice," he said, his voice already sounding far away. "Mmm, you smell so good...."

Beshel paused. His nostrils flared as he breathed in. Underneath the scent of his semen, under the smell of Peri's, he detected what Peri was talking about. He hadn't even realized his body had released the chemical pheromones.

Not wanting to think about what that meant, Beshel continued his clean up. After wiping his dripping cock, he tossed the dirty garment onto the floor. Crawling into bed, Beshel lay down next to Peri. Despite the fact his swollen erection was still hard and throbbing, he pulled his boy close. Peri snuggled back into him and immediately began to softly snuffle against the pillow.

Beshel's erection pulsated again, and more semen oozed out of the slit, dripping against the smooth round cheeks of Peri's ass. The pressure was almost unbearably painful, and instinctually he knew the only way to relieve it would be to bury his cock back inside Peri's ass.

He grit his teeth, bearing the discomfort, while trying not to think about what was happening, what this meant. Just when he thought he couldn't take any more and would need to go into the bathroom to take care of himself manually, his cock began to soften, and the pressure dissipated.

Letting out a relieved breath, Beshel finally closed his eyes.

* * * *

The sound of a communication chime interrupted their brief nap.

Beshel sat up. "Stay here. I'll find out what's going on."

"Chief Drago, this is Captain Bragman. Report to the bridge."

Chapter 19

"Based on the trajectory, the ship is headed toward this star system, Gliese 646."

Beshel watched as Kenji pointed toward the monitor, his finger tracing the computer generated path.

"There is a mining outpost on the largest moon of the fourth planet." Kenji double-tapped the screen, and the computer zoomed in on the planet, then its moon. A blinking square indicated the location of the outpost.

Captain Bragman leaned in closer. "What do we know about this system?"

"Geographically, it's inside Union borders, though none of the planets in the Gliese system are habitable. The lunar outpost attached to the mine has a self-contained biosphere. The Union database indicates the outpost has been abandoned for the past ten years."

The captain turned to the helmsman, a red-skinned Regulan. "Lieutenant Kasix, set an intercept course. Don't let them reach that outpost."

"Yes, sir." Kasix immediately changed course and engaged the engines.

"Lieutenant." He addressed Kenji. "Jam their transmissions. I don't want them alerting their friends just yet."

"Yes, sir."

"And scan the system for any other vessels. When we get close enough to the outpost, scan for lifesigns. I want to know what we're dealing with."

The captain took his chair.

Beshel was impressed with Captain Bragman so far. He was

doing everything he'd have done if he were in command. He'd never worked with a Sargan before. One of the founding species of the Galactic Planetary Union, they had a reputation for quick thinking and advanced analysis.

He followed Corporal Durant to the weapons station.

"So, I take it the embryo belongs to the kid?" Durant asked quietly as he activated his workstation.

"Yes. Peri is the father. Though it's grown quite a bit since we saw the original photo-scans taken after its recovery. It's no longer an embryo."

"So, the not-an-embryo belongs to Peri... and Peri belongs to you?"

"He's not my property, if that's what you're asking."

"You know damn well what I'm—"

An alarm sounded from Durant's workstation, accompanied by a flashing control. "Shit," the security officer murmured. He tapped the flashing button.

Beshel watched the bridge's main viewscreen come to life. A small ship appeared on the screen. It was too small to positively identify, but to Beshel it looked like an older class Union ship.

"Magnify image," Bragman ordered. "Is the ship broadcasting an identification signal?"

"Negative," Kenji responded. "They've disabled their transponder. It's a common mod used by pirates."

"Tactical analysis?"

Corporal Durant's fingers flew across his terminal. The computer scanned the vessel's configuration, and the ship blueprints and schematics came up after only a couple of seconds. The view screen zoomed in on the vessel. "Old Union *Beta*-class raider. It's been a while since I've seen one of these bad boys. Engines appear to have been retrofitted, since it's moving faster than its original rated speed. Based on its energy signatures, I'd say the weapons have been refit as well."

Bragman tapped a button on his chair, activating the ship-wide comm system. "This is the Captain. All hands to battle stations. This is not a drill. All hands to battle stations."

The *Artemis* quickly gained on the smaller ship.

"Open comm," Bragman ordered.

Kenji activated the communications system. "Channel open. Broadcasting all frequencies."

"This is Captain Bragman, commanding officer, U.S.C. *Artemis*. Stand down immediately, and prepare to be boarded."

Abruptly the fighter turned in a one-eighty and headed straight for the *Artemis*.

"If that's the way they want to play it… Corporal, prepare weapons."

Beshel tensed. The *Artemis* could easily destroy the rogue vessel, and with it, the baby. He'd made Peri a promise, and he intended to keep it. Opening his mouth, he was about to interrupt the captain.

The Captain swiveled in his chair and glanced at Durant before looking at Beshel. "We want the ship intact. We have precious cargo to retrieve."

Beshel gave the Captain a nod in acknowledgement.

"Torpedo!" Durant called out. "Brace for impact!"

The viewscreen image displayed a red circle surrounding the torpedo, which sailed toward the ship at high velocity. A graphical schematic of the torpedo displayed in the corner, showing its armament and yield.

"Return fire!" Captain Bragman commanded.

Beshel drew in a breath and held it as Durant carried out the captain's orders. A pair of torpedoes launched from the *Artemis*.

The raider's torpedo hit the ship, and the *Artemis* shuddered from the impact, but she easily held together.

"Shields holding," Kenji reported.

Beshel watched the screen as one of the torpedoes made

contact with the pirate ship. The other missed, but the single hit was enough to cause the ship to slow.

Durant tapped his terminal controls. "Targeting engines. Firing particle weapons."

The particle beams hit the ship, and with a quick flash of light and smoke, it came to a full stop. The motion dampeners must have been affected by the blast, as the ship began a sluggish roll to starboard.

Bragman turned to Durant. "Corporal, prepare a boarding party."

* * * *

Peri watched the battle from the viewport of his and Besh's quarters. Thank god, they had accommodations at the front of the ship. It was like a front row seat at the movies.

He felt an explosion hit the ship, and he grabbed the wall to steady himself.

His heart pounded in his chest as he watched the *Artemis* blast the humans' ship with laser beams. They were going to kill his baby!

Within moments, the battle seemed over from what Peri could see from the window. The ship turned, and the kidnappers' vessel began to move out of view. He wondered if there was another place on the ship with a better vantage point.

The *Artemis* seemed to be moving in very close. When it began to tilt to line up with the other starship, Peri realized they were going to physically dock. That meant they were going to send a boarding party into the pirate ship.

No way in hell was he going to just stand by. He had to get on that ship, and he had to get his baby.

Ignoring the desperate need for a shower, he hurriedly dressed, sliding into a pair of black pants and a matching black shirt. He pulled on his boots and left the room. After checking with a computer console, he found out where the ship's docking port was located.

When he arrived at the airlock, Beshel, Martan, Kenji, Durant and the *Artemis* security crew were standing outside the door waiting for the airlock to pressurize. Durant handed comm units to Beshel and Martan, and they looped them around their ears. The devices were similar to what he'd used when he worked at the spaceport.

When Beshel turned and saw Peri, he stopped him. "What are you doing here? I told you to wait in our quarters."

"I'm coming with you."

Beshel ground his teeth. "No, you're not."

"You can't tell me 'no.' I need to make sure he is okay."

"I promised you I would bring him back."

"Beshel, please. We've come this far. I'll do whatever you say."

Beshel turned toward Durant, who shook his head with a sigh. "The kid's your responsibility." Durant tossed Peri a comm unit.

Peri caught it. "And I'm not a kid," he snapped back. He looped it over his left ear, and pressed it into his ear canal, then adjusted the boom mic.

"Stay behind me," Beshel warned. Peri opened his mouth to retort, but Beshel cut him off with a finger. "If we run into any trouble, I want you to head back to the *Artemis*. I won't negotiate on this."

"But—"

Kenji interrupted. "Actually, I could use his help." He was carrying an unwieldy black plastic box, emblazoned with the Union Medical logo. He lifted the box up by the handle. "We'll need to transfer the hybrid—uh, baby—into this incubation unit. It'll take the both of us."

Peri smiled at the scientist. He knew Kenji was exaggerating, but he was grateful for the excuse, lame as it was. "Thank you."

Martan took the unit from Kenji. "Let me help you with this, Kenji."

"Thank you, Martan." Kenji smiled shyly and turned away. A blush crept up his cheeks as he pulled his comPad from his uniform and fiddled with it.

When the airlock pressurized, Durant drew his pistol. "I want everyone on their A-game. We need to locate the cargo, and get back to the ship."

One of the Artemis security officers cut through the rogue ship's airlock with a blast welder, then blew the door. As soon as the door fell to the ground with a loud *clang*, weapons fire erupted.

The officer manning the welding torch slumped to the ground, his eyes wide open, lifeless. Particle weapons had blasted a smoldering hole in the middle of his chest.

Peri covered his mouth to keep from gagging.

The *Artemis* crew returned fire, advancing through the door, taking out any resistance they encountered.

Peri was surprised to see the kidnappers were indeed human, and they wore Union uniforms. In the back of his head, he'd hoped what they'd said on the news wasn't true.

Kenji scanned one of the dead kidnappers with his comPad. "He's wearing a Union Navy uniform, but he's not Union Navy. He doesn't have a cranial implant chip." He tapped the back of his neck at the base of his skull, where Peri assumed he had an implant of his own.

"Could he have had it removed or deactivated?" Durant asked.

Kenji shook his head. "I don't think so. There doesn't seem to be any scar tissue that would've remained from what should be the implant site, or from its removal."

"Get a DNA sample from each of these assholes. Once we get back to the ship, we'll try to ID them."

Once Kenji—covered by Martan—collected the samples and cataloged them, he pointed toward the right hallway. "This way."

Corporal Durant and his men took lead, and they maneuvered through the corridors swiftly, easily taking out any pirates they encountered.

"In here." Kenji stopped outside a door marked "Med Bay."

Durant looked toward his officers. "Ready? Go." He activated the door control.

As they slid open, his team moved through. Particle weapons fired, and Peri jumped back, with Beshel covering him with his bigger body.

"Man down!" Durant shouted as he dragged another Marine from the doorway. He dropped to a roll, and then fired his rifle. He and the remaining security officers advanced.

Keeping his word, Peri stayed with Kenji behind Beshel and Martan.

After Durant announced, "All clear," Peri followed Kenji and Beshel into the med bay.

The room was filled with smoke, making it slightly difficult to get his bearings.

"Over here!" Kenji raced to one of the biobeds. The Degan incubator sat on top of the bed. Its cables connected it to the old computer system with a series of hot-wired adapters.

Peri went to help him while Durant spoke with Beshel. "We'll clear the rest of the ship. Get back to the *Artemis* as soon as you can."

"Try to capture at least one of the pirates alive, Corporal."

Durant snickered. "I'll do my best, Chief."

Peri watched the incubator unit's lights blinking rapidly. A high-pitched noise beeped in a staccato rhythm.

"What's wrong?" Peri asked Kenji.

"The unit is failing," Kenji answered. "It must've been damaged in the battle."

"Oh god. Can you fix it?"

Kenji tapped at the controls. "No. Get the new unit set up. Hurry, Martan."

Martan opened the case and removed the unit he brought over from the *Artemis*, sitting it next to the failing unit. No sooner had he set the unit up when the broken unit cracked open and began to leak pink fluid all over the bed.

Peri gasped, rushing forward to place his hand over the leak. Beshel was behind him, pulling Peri to his chest, enveloping him in his furred arms. "Besh, no!"

They couldn't have gotten this far, only to lose their child. It wasn't fair.

"Let them do their job, Peri."

Kenji snapped on a pair of surgical gloves. He reached into the incubation unit. When he pulled his cupped hands out, the baby was cradled in his palms.

Peri gasped at the baby's size. Now the size of a softball, he was easily twice as big as when he'd seen him last. He looked like a small human baby... if you ignored the big button nose, cranial horn nubs, and the tail. The top of the baby's head was already covered in fine black hair, just like Peri's. His eyes were closed, so Peri couldn't see what color they were. He really hoped they were green like Besh's.

He felt Beshel's body go rigid behind him. "My gods," he whispered.

Then Peri realized something wasn't right. Curled up in a ball, the baby didn't seem to be moving. Its skin was pink, but had an odd blue tint to it. That wasn't right. He shouldn't be blue. And he should be moving.

Why wasn't he moving?

After Kenji placed the baby into the new unit, he tapped a button. The unit sealed shut and it filled with fluid.

The new unit's display panel activated, and the screen displayed *Calibrating vital signs.*

After a moment, the display cleared.

Vital signs calibrated. Unit online.

A steady flatline tone sounded, filling the room with the harsh noise.

No.

No!

Peri's knees buckled, but Besh was there to hold him up. That didn't stop the wail that burst from his chest. Besh cradled Peri, pulling him back tight, as Peri sobbed uncontrollably. The sound of his crying drowned out the damned noise. The noise that signaled the death of his child.

It wasn't fair. What had his child done to deserve this? He was innocent. They hadn't even had a chance to name him. His baby had died nameless and alone.

"Peri...."

If they'd gotten here sooner, then maybe they could've saved him. If Beshel had listened to him earlier, when he begged them to leave. Hot tears clogged his eyes, blurring everything around him. He could feel Beshel's arms around him, but everything else felt numb. Beshel had given his word, and he hadn't kept it. Another round of sobs began.

Peri turned and slammed his fists into Beshel's chest, hitting the alien beast as hard as he could. "You promised!"

"Peri!"

Beshel grabbed Peri's wrists, and Peri screamed as he struggled, trying to pull away. He had to get out of there. He couldn't listen to that sound anymore.

When Peri didn't respond, Beshel shook him. The action was firm, not enough to hurt, but enough to get Peri's attention. "Peri. *Listen.*"

The machine's dreadful noise had abruptly stopped. A single beep was emitted, short and quiet. It was followed by another... then another...

Kenji blew out a breath, then sniffled. "Everything is okay."

"It is?"

Peri hiccupped, then wiped his tears and his nose with his sleeve. He and Beshel looked into the new unit. Still curled in a small ball, their baby floated in the liquid. His fists uncurled and curled. He opened his mouth as if yawning.

"*Strike team.*" The Captain's voice filtered through his earpiece. "*Get back to the ship immediately. Two ships are closing on our position.*"

Chapter 20

While Peri rushed off with Kenji to get the baby set up in sickbay, Beshel reluctantly headed to the bridge with Corporal Durant. The ship was still on alert, and the activity in the corridors reflected that. He was torn between his duty and leaving Peri and the baby, but he knew he would be more useful at the ship's command center.

"No response from the lunar biosphere, Captain," the officer at the comm station announced.

"They hear us," the Captain said as he looked fixedly at the empty viewscreen. "They know we're here. Cease transmission."

Durant relieved the officer at the tactical station.

Bragman stood and turned toward tactical. "Welcome back, Corporal."

"Captain. Our mission was a success."

"Excellent. Helm, begin undocking procedures immediately. Move us away from the raider." He turned back to Durant. "Do we have identification on the two approaching ships?"

"They're coming in range now, Captain." Durant switched the bridge's main viewscreen to display the tactical sensor grid. "They're coming in hot."

On the viewer, two generic icons rapidly closed in toward the center of the screen, where the U.S.C. *Artemis* was depicted as an icon model of an *Epsilon*-class cruiser, with the ship's name and unique transponder registry appearing under it in text.

One of the approaching icons flashed as it came into range, and its transponder data appeared: "U.S.C. *Cassini* Mark II." The icon changed to depict a *Zeta*-class Union cruiser. Immediately after it, the other ship was identified: "D.N.S. *Akbal.*"

All heads turned toward Beshel. The *Akbal* was a Degan Navy battleship. One of the fleet's biggest. It had more than enough firepower to take on both Union ships.

The Captain cleared his throat. "Open comm to the *Cassini*."

Durant followed through with the order, and a dark-skinned human male appeared on the viewscreen.

"Captain Yoruba, is there something I can help you with?" Bragman asked politely.

"Captain Bragman. I was about to ask you the same thing. I have Dr. Adler here, to provide assistance to Lieutenant Kanataka and the hybrid child."

"And your *escort*?"

"Ah. The Degans are convinced we were involved in the attack on their science institute. They say they have evidence Dr. Adler is working with the rogue scientists."

"That's just ridiculous."

Yoruba smirked. "Yes, I am aware. He's the one who originally rescued the child from the scientists and helped to destroy their lab."

"We believe the rogue scientists have set up camp at the lunar mining outpost. We should pool resources."

"It's imperative we take these men into custody. We could stop this war before it starts."

Beshel interrupted the two commanding officers, moving to stand by Bragman's side. "Captain Yoruba, I apologize for interrupting. I am the Degan Federation's Chief Investigator Beshel Drago. Perhaps I could speak with the *Akbal*'s captain, and convince him to join us."

"I welcome any aid you could provide, Chief Drago."

Once Durant opened a comm link to the *Akbal*, Beshel identified himself. They did not respond. Beshel repeated his transmission. After a few tense moments, the *Akbal* finally established a two-way video link.

The Degan captain's image appeared on the viewscreen.

"Captain, I am—"

"Yes, I'm aware of who you are, Chief Investigator. You have been declared AWOL by our government. How interesting to find you conspiring with the enemy."

"You have me at a disadvantage, Captain…."

"Teldo."

"Captain Teldo, these men and women are not our enemy. You'll find the real enemy on the raider, and on the outpost located on the largest moon of the fourth planet. Time is of the essence, Captain. We must capture these rogues before they escape."

"And how do I know that *you* are not here to help them escape?"

"Captain, we've recovered the stolen child." Beshel sighed. "*My* child."

"*Your* child?"

"Yes. I am his sire."

Captain Teldo leaned forward in his chair and stared at Beshel with a scrutinizing eye. After a long silence, he leaned back in his chair. "I am inclined to believe you. But I will send an investigative team to the raider to corroborate your findings, and two members of my prime security teams will accompany you on the outpost raid."

Beshel glanced at Captain Bragman, who nodded his agreement. "Your terms are acceptable."

"Do not even think of deception, or you will suffer the full wrath of this battleship."

Teldo cut transmission.

* * * *

Beshel double-checked he had his phase-pistol set to *kill*, and holstered it. He then checked his comm ear piece.

Next to him, Durant did the same with a smirk on his face. "Remember, we're trying to take these guys alive, Chief."

"Right," he growled. "Alive."

The shuttle bay's ready room bustled with activity as the strike team prepared to depart the *Artemis*. In addition to Beshel and Martan, Durant and two of his security team members would travel down to the lunar surface via shuttle, which would be piloted by Regulan Lieutenant Kasix. Two security officers from the *Cassini* were en route to join them, one of them Kane Robertson. Both *Cassini* officers had served on the mission to XP-8460, where the embryo—Beshel's offspring—was retrieved. Their experience with the rogue scientist's weapons and cyborgs would hopefully prove to be valuable to the strike team.

Beshel performed a series of stretches to loosen his muscles. It had been a while since he'd been on an offensive op. Even longer since he'd had to wear an EV suit. The environmental suit Durant provided him was snug on his large frame, but it was lightweight and flexible while still being durable and space-ready.

Underneath the EV, he wore a Union-issued full-body singlet. The pitch-black elastic garment hugged every nook and cranny of his body, but would keep him warm and dry under the EV suit. Peri said it made him look like a bad ass ninja, whatever that was. Clearly it was a good thing, because Peri was visibly turned on when Beshel got dressed.

"You look good in a Union Marine EV uniform, Chief. You should enlist."

"Bite your tongue, mister."

Durant laughed. He reached into the weapons locker and pulled out a standard issue phase rifle. "Here. Try this. I think it might be more to your size."

Beshel gripped the rifle with both hands. It was a good size, and had a hefty, heavy grip. "Yes, this will do nicely."

"That baby's got ten times the firepower of the handhelds."

Beshel nodded his thanks as he strapped the rifle over his shoulder.

"Don't say I never gave you nothin'," he replied with a snicker. He went down the line, checking the rest of his team.

Martan pulled Beshel aside. "My leave has been canceled. I've been recalled to the *Kaba*. I just received the orders via comm. I'm supposed to report by tomorrow morning. I've requested emergency leave for family reasons, but I doubt it will be approved."

Beshel placed his hand on Martan's shoulder and gave a gentle squeeze. "I'll do what I can, as I'm sure your parents will."

"I don't know if it will help, to be honest. Uncle Besh, they're deploying the naval fleet, setting up blockades along our borders. I know I'm doing the right thing being here, but I don't want to be branded a wartime deserter."

"That will not happen, Martan."

Once everyone was nearly suited up and ready, Captain Bragman entered with two officers.

"Team, this is Sergeant Robertson and Lieutenant Yates of the *Cassini*. Robertson is senior officer. He'll be in charge, coordinating with Corporal Durant and Degan Lieutenant Elbar."

The enhanced human stepped forward. Clapping his hands behind his back, he spread his legs shoulder width apart. Even though he was *at ease*, he appeared dangerous and powerful, standing ramrod straight. "I'm Sergeant Kane Robertson. I've sent our data to your tactical chiefs. I hope by now you've all had a chance to review the data on the hybrid cyborgs, as well as upgrade your weapons. Our sensors aren't picking anything up right now, but given our last run-in with these assholes, you can assume they've got some tricks up their sleeves."

"Thank you, Sergeant." Bragman stopped. He let out a tired breath. "Two more Degan battleships are closing in on our location, and they are not coming to help. I don't need to tell you what's at stake. We capture these men, we prevent a war. I'll see you all when you return. Get to it."

* * * *

"Peri, where are you going?" Kenji asked as he chased after Peri.

Peri didn't stop. He hurried through the corridor, looking back at Kenji. "I need to tell Besh something before he leaves."

Kenji increased his pace to catch up. "The shuttle bay ready room and armory are off-limits. You'll need a crew member to escort you."

Peri glanced at Kenji, noting the small smile on his face. *Escort, my ass.*

He entered the shuttle bay just in time. The strike team was already dressed in their space suits and they were getting ready to board the shuttle. From the back, Beshel looked pretty damn good. He held his helmet in one hand, and had a huge-ass rifle slung over his shoulder.

Peri's eyes drifted down the broad back to his trim waist, which flared out in a bubble butt you could eat breakfast off of. The space suit was tight on him, and it served to show off his assets. As Beshel turned, Peri got a nice view of his package. Lifting his eyes, Peri found the Degan's face contorted into an angry scowl.

"Peri," he snarled. "Absolutely not!"

Peri grabbed Beshel's hand and pulled him off to the side, where he would have a bit of privacy from the other men.

"I know I can't come with you," Peri said quietly. "But I had to tell you something before you left."

Wrapping his fingers around the collar of Beshel's space suit, he gave a tug down until Beshel's head was within reach. Pushing up on his tiptoes, Peri placed a soft kiss on Beshel's lips.

"Please come back. I need you. *We* need you."

Peri wanted to tell Besh more, but he didn't think it was the right time. The most important thing was Beshel knowing how much Peri and their baby needed him.

Beshel pulled Peri into a bear hug. He covered his mouth and sealed it with a blistering kiss. When he ended the kiss, he still held onto Peri for a moment longer.

Rubbing his nose in Peri's hair, breathing deeply, he said softly, "I promise."

* * * *

Two shuttles, one from the *Artemis* and one from the *Akbal,* carried the strike teams to the lunar surface.

Beshel sat ramrod straight in his chair, mentally preparing himself for the upcoming battle. The enormity of the situation threatened to overwhelm him. He hadn't realized until the baby had nearly died how *real* this was. If he let his anger get the better of him, he'd fuck up the op. For now, he needed to detach himself from the situation and concentrate on successfully apprehending these criminals and bringing them to justice. Not just for Peri and their child, but for the entire galaxy.

Suddenly feeling calm, Beshel glanced out the nearest porthole, searching for their destination.

The mining colony building was located at the foot of a mountain range, on a relatively flat plateau. Beacon lights illuminated the landing pad, which was large enough to land a mid-sized space cruiser. Two shuttles would be no problem.

The lack of breathable atmosphere kept the surface dark; the star was far enough away the light it gave would not be much more than what was cast by Dega's full moon at night.

The Degan shuttle was in the lead. It broke formation to line up with the power generators. One torpedo destroyed the generator and severed the power link. The colony's lights went completely black, including the landing beacons. Within seconds, the beacons flickered back to life, at half illumination, as the backup generators kicked in.

Once Lieutenant Kasix set the ship down, the team pulled their EV helmets on and secured them.

Corporal Durant's voice filtered in through Beshel's earpiece. "Comm check." Once the entire team responded, Durant checked each man's EV suit.

"Durant to *Artemis*. Strike Team's EV systems are online; ox levels and seals read optimal."

"*Copy that, Corporal. We're reading the team one hundred percent,*" Bragman replied from the *Artemis*. "*Good luck.*"

"Durant to Elbar. *Artemis* strike team ready to go."

On Robertson's command, Durant opened the airlock.

Beshel followed him down the ramp.

* * * *

The Artemis strike team was joined by three Degans from the *Akbal.* The combined strike team convened on the colony's main airlock door. The pair of massive metal doors were large enough to drive a tank through. Once they got inside the doors and sealed them shut, they'd need to pressurize it before they could enter the building proper.

The infernal EV helmet limited Beshel's field of vision somewhat, so he scanned his surroundings with great vigilance. Elbar and the Degan strike team took up the rear, facing out, searching for threats. The young human from the *Cassini* was already at the blast doors, working on opening the airlock.

The biosphere structure looked old and outdated.

If one didn't take note of the new beacon lights outlining the landing strip and the modern, sophisticated airlock panel, one might have thought it was still abandoned.

"I got a bad feeling about this," one of the men whispered over comm—Private Samuels.

"It's too quiet," Martan whispered.

Beshel agreed, but at the same time, he was eager to get in there. They'd capture these men, and end these experiments for good.

Robertson's voice sounded in Beshel's ear. "Open the door on my mark. Three... two... one... mark."

A shower of sparks and a small-scale explosion took out the door control. The outer airlock door began to slide open, metal gears grinding hard enough Beshel felt the vibrations through his boots. They jerked to a stop and the vibrations abruptly ceased.

If the scientists hadn't known before about the strike teams, they sure did now.

Robertson turned to the young human at his side. "Lieutenant Yates, scan the structure."

Yates scanned the area with his pad. "The airlock scans empty, Sarge." He smacked the plastic comPad against his fist, then tried to scan again. "Hell. *Everything* is scanning empty. They must have a dampening field."

Kasix, the Regulan pilot, held up his pad. "I'm reading nothing as well. It's like a big black box."

Though he wasn't in command, Beshel spoke up, his voice-actuated microphone broadcasting to the rest of the team. "Sergeant, if all ten of us enter that airlock, we're sitting ducks while we wait for it to pressurize. They could blast us into space."

"You're right, Chief," Robertson answered. "Yates, Kasix. Any other ways into the structure?"

Holding his pad in front of him, Kasix brought up the biosphere's outside blueprints. The red-skinned alien walked down the length of the building, then returned. "There's a service port on the east side. The tunnel leads down one level to a smaller maintenance airlock. It looks like it's still operational."

Robertson turned toward Durant. "Corporal, take a team through the service port. The rest of us will go in through the main door. Keep your comm open. Let us know if you run into any opposition."

"Yes, sir," Durant replied. He turned toward Beshel and Martan. "Chief, Lieutenant, you're with me. You too, Donovan."

The private eagerly saluted and joined up with Martan and Beshel.

"We'll rendezvous in the atrium, just inside the main airlock."

"Let's go, team."

Beshel and Martan followed Durant to the service port. The service port was a cylindrical, vertical conduit. Covered with a metal hatch, water condensation escaped from a pair of fist-sized holes, the vapor disappearing into the dark sky.

"Stand back." Durant aimed his phase pistol. With one accurate blast, he blew off the hinge. Beshel stepped forward and helped him push the hatch cover off the conduit.

He aimed the light strapped to his forearm down into the port. The light wasn't strong enough to see the bottom of the structure. A series of metal bars arranged down the cylinder served as a ladder. It was going to be a tight fit for someone of Beshel's size, but he wouldn't have a problem. He turned to his nephew. "You're not claustrophobic, are you?"

"No, sir," Martan replied.

"I'll take point," Durant announced. "Chief, take the rear."

Durant climbed into the service port and began his descent. Donovan and Martan followed him in.

The climb down was a little further than Beshel thought it would be. By the time he reached the bottom, his arm muscles were starting to tire. The atrium at the bottom of the service port was a tight fit for all four team members. Donovan was already at the airlock panel, attempting to override the security lock for the door's manual lever.

Water vapor and gasses flowed into the crowded space from various pipes and outlets, heading for the surface.

Beshel used his gloved hand to wipe off the condensation gathering on the front of his helmet.

"Hurry up, Private," Durant pushed.

The tip of Donovan's tongue poked out the side of his mouth as he concentrated on what he was doing. "Just about got it..."

The panel beeped. Donovan grabbed the override lever. With a strained grunt, he pulled the lever down and locked it into the open position. The outer airlock door opened with a hiss as the cooler air inside blasted through the opening. It combined with the condensation vapor, swirling up the conduit toward the surface.

"Durant to Robertson. We're going in."

"*Roger that.*"

Once inside, Donovan sealed the hatch and initiated pressurization.

"Weapons ready," Durant ordered, turning to face the inner door.

Beshel drew his phase pistol, disengaged the safety, and made sure once again it was set to *kill.*

It seemed as if the pressurization cycle took way longer than it should, but that was probably Beshel's imagination.

As soon as the airlock reached one hundred percent, Durant counted down, giving time for everyone to get ready. He hit the inner control panel. The door opened and the team quickly moved out in formation, weapons drawn.

The corridor was dark, save for the flashing strobe light above the airlock door. Ceiling-mounted emergency lights lit up doorways with an eerie red cast. Other than that, the only illumination came from the team's forearm-mounted flashlights.

The sound of the others breathing in his earpiece was almost enough to distract Beshel from focusing on his surroundings.

"Scanner is clear," Donovan quietly announced. "The stairwell is up to the right, ten meters."

"Keep formation tight. Keep your eyes and ears open," Durant ordered. "Scanners might not be reliable in here."

It was too quiet for Beshel. They should have been met with some kind of resistance. Surely the scientists were aware of the strike team's presence.

Just as they began moving toward the stairwell, Beshel picked up a foreign sound. An odd buzzing from somewhere in the dark. Before he could say anything, Durant ordered the team to hold position.

"You hear it too?" Beshel whispered.

Durant nodded, then turned to try to identify the source. Beshel did the same.

"I don't hear anything," Private Donovan added. He slapped his pad against his rifle and held it up. "I don't see anything either."

The sound grew louder. A mechanical whirring noise added to the buzz.

"Over here!" Martan shouted as he turned and crouched. He aimed his forearm toward the ceiling, letting his flashlight illuminate the source.

The beam of light hit an ovoid-shaped object, about two feet in diameter, propelling itself through the air like a mini hovercar. A multitude of mechanical appendages hung from its smooth metallic body like tentacles, each one ending in a different tool of some sort. It had a series of eight organic eyes on what Beshel would consider the front of the droid. Each of them had familiar emerald green irises, each staring off in a different direction. One of them was trained directly on Beshel. With pupils blown wide open, it was like staring into an abyss.

A shudder ran through Beshel's body.

Beshel changed the angle of his light. The droid was not alone. Ten more followed it, all of them whirring down the hallway in a reversed V formation.

"Fire!" Durant ordered.

Beshel didn't have to be told twice. He fired his phase pistol directly at the ovoid's evil eye. Two more shots and the flying abomination fell to the ground, letting out an inhuman shriek before it exploded.

The closest spider-bot lifted one of its appendages. A blue light shot out of the tool, a wide beam that engulfed the entire strike team. Beshel could feel the warmth of the scanner even through his EV suit.

Martan shot at the bot, hitting it several times before it fell to the floor in a smoldering heap.

The remaining bots split into two groups, one close to the ceiling, and one closer to the floor. They dodged the strike team's weapons fire, moving in an undulating, seemingly-random formation, zigging and zagging, rising and falling, slowing down and speeding up.

The team fired repeatedly, trying to predict their movements.

Beshel suddenly noticed Martan had several pinpoints of red illuminating the front of his EV suit. The droids had selected his nephew with laser targets. He quickly glanced around at the rest of the team, and found no other targets. When he looked down at his own chest, he found a swirling swarm of laser beams pointing at his chest.

"Martan!" Beshel shouted as he threw himself to the floor. "Get down! Fall back!"

It was too late.

Half of the droids opened fire on Martan, hitting him square in the chest. He went down with a stifled grunt. Before Beshel could retrieve his nephew, one of the droids shot a rope from one of its appendages. The white rope—resembling a spider's web—snared Martan's foot. Another droid did the same.

A barrage of web netting flew in all directions at the team members, accompanied by particle beams.

Beshel's eardrum was nearly blown out when Donovan screamed into his microphone. The distressed cry was abruptly silenced.

Beshel rolled, but one of the nets hit his side, knocking him backward to the floor. Lying flat on his back, he adjusted his rifle's intensity setting to max. Aiming at the closest droid, he fired. A second shot and the bot exploded in a shower of sparks and metal fragments. A foul-smelling splattering of dark goo smeared the wall and floor.

"Set your weapons on max," Beshel shouted into his mic.

Again and again, Beshel fired until the rifle finally overloaded and shut down.

While the team was busy destroying the bots, the two droids that had snared Martan dragged him down the hall, disappearing in the darkness.

Chapter 21

"No!" Beshel screamed.

His rifle was useless. He tossed the overheated hunk of metal to the ground and drew his pistol. Aiming his flashlight down the hallway, he began a brisk walk, aiming his light in every direction, search for any sign of the bots that had taken Martan.

"Drago, wait!" Durant shouted.

Reluctantly, Beshel stopped and turned toward Durant. "What?"

"We need to meet up with the others."

"Those things have my nephew!"

"We've lost Private Donovan, and Martan—"

"We did *not* lose Martan!"

"Chief, it's just the two of us. We don't know what else is out there. We need to regroup with the others."

Beshel used his flashlight, and aimed it behind Durant, illuminating an obscure shadow. The *Artemis* security officer was snared in a web, pinned to the corridor floor. The face shield of Donovan's EV helmet had been burned open by a particle weapon.

He averted the light, not wanting to see the damage the spider-bots had done to the man.

"We'll get him back, Beshel," Durant said softly. "You have my word."

Beshel let out a hard breath and holstered his weapon. The human was right. He wouldn't be able to find his nephew alone. They stood a better chance with the entire strike force. Walking over to Donovan, he squatted down and pulled the phase rifle from the hands of the dead human. "Fine," he said as he ratcheted up the setting to *max*.

Durant nodded. "Durant to Robertson. What's your status?"

"*Go ahead, corporal.*"

"We're inside. We encountered resistance from a swarm of spider-bots. I've lost a man, and Lieutenant Drago has been taken captive."

"*Did you say spider-bots?*"

"Yeah, that's what I said."

"*What the fuck. It's quiet here. Meet us at the rendezvous point ASAP.*"

"We're on our way. Watch your back."

* * * *

Peri watched Kenji operate the sensor controls on his workstation. Folding his arms across his chest, he brought his hand up to his mouth and began to nibble on his thumbnail.

The *Artemis* operating system was far more sophisticated than what he was used to when he worked at Spaceport Prime on Earth. Still, it was familiar enough that he got the gist of what Kenji was doing.

Kenji was trying to break through the scanning blocks on the mining colony. If he was successful, then they would be able to give a heads up to the strike team.

"Damn it," Kenji muttered to himself.

"What's wrong?" Peri asked. He moved closer so he could see the screen better.

"I've tried all combinations of the sensor dampeners they were using on XP-8460. I'm still unable to get a clear reading of what's inside the main structure. They must have upgraded their dampening technology."

"Damn."

Kenji reached over and tapped a button on his upper workstation screen. "Connect to Dr. Aron Adler, U.S.C. *Cassini*."

A few seconds later, Aron's video link appeared on the screen. "Kenji, Peri. Nice to see you both again. I only wish it was under better circumstances."

"Me, too," Peri agreed.

Kenji nodded along. "Aron, I've been working on trying to break the scanner dampeners, but I haven't had any luck."

"I'm doing the same over here. I have some ideas, though. I just need some time."

"We should work together. Maybe we can break it quicker, with both of us working on it."

"That's what I was thinking. I'll get permission from the captain to join you on the *Artemis*. I would like to check on our little patient as well."

* * * *

"Hold your fire!" Durant shouted. "It's us."

Beshel and Durant stepped out into the atrium, hands out. Robertson and Elbar's teams lowered their weapons. Beshel immediately noticed that the strike team and the Degans had removed their EV suits.

The visual alarm over the atrium's airlock door was still blinking. The strobe effect was enough to give Beshel a headache. There was no other light in the room, not even emergency lighting.

"Report, Corporal," Robertson ordered.

Durant unlocked his helmet, then removed it. He drew in a cautious breath, then let it out. "We lost Donovan, and Lieutenant Drago was taken by spider-bots. It took several hits to completely destroy them, but the max setting on the phase rifles could get them in one or two shots. Unfortunately, they tend to overheat when fired too many times without a break."

Beshel popped the latch on his helmet and got rid of his EV suit. Taking in a deep breath, he let it out slowly. He'd expected the air to be stale, as it would be if this was indeed an abandoned facility. Obviously, the ventilation system was operational and was circulating clean air. He set his suit aside with the others.

"They didn't choose him randomly," Beshel added to Durant's report. "They scanned us, then targeted Martan and myself with the webs." He glanced over at Elbar and his team. "Watch yourselves. These people want our kind."

Elbar sneered, exposing his sharp canine teeth. "Let them come for us." He lifted his rifle and rested it on his shoulder.

Beshel sincerely hoped Elbar's bravado wouldn't get him killed. Or worse.

* * * *

Aron let out an annoyed sigh. The exobiologist had quickly reached the point of frustration. Peri didn't blame him. The man's husband was down on that rock. A sitting duck, just like Beshel and the others.

The scientist managed to connect to the lunar colony mainframe. The original computer network was still up and running, but it appeared they'd added modern security to it. Since that was a dead end, he instead concentrated his efforts on the jammer technology.

"I thought their scanner jammers would be based on the Crixan reptile-based technology that they used on the XP-8460 prototypes. It seems that they've been busy upgrading."

Kenji skimmed through the data on the screen. "Maybe they couldn't apply the Crixan technology on such a large scale. Or maybe this facility was in use *before* they adapted your research."

Peri had no idea what they were talking about, but it sounded like they were over-thinking it. "Maybe you should just hack into their system and turn it off."

Aron turned in his seat to face Peri. "Interesting. Is that a skillset you possess?"

Peri grimaced. "No. It was just a suggestion. Can't you do it?"

"I'm a biologist, not a cyber-hacker."

Kenji huffed. "Too bad your buddy Bradley Brimley's in prison. I'm sure he could help."

"He's not my *buddy*, seeing how he tried to kill me and all."

Kenji and Aron snickered, though Peri didn't really get the reference. After a moment, Aron lit up. "But you know what? Maybe your idea that this is an *older* facility has some merit."

"What do you mean?" Kenji asked.

Aron was too busy digging through files on the computer to answer directly. "I know I have some of Bradley's personal data in my archives somewhere," he said to himself. "Here they are."

Peri watched Aron sift and search through file after file.

"I think this is it."

Kenji leaned forward and looked at the file directory's header. "What's E.L.M.?"

"No clue," Aron answered.

Peri shook his head. "I've never heard of it either."

"The directory contains a bunch of coded files, but there's no context. I remember thinking they looked like security credentials though."

Peri pointed to the screen. "What about that one? It starts with MCG646, and we're in the Gliese 646 system."

"I don't know. It can't be that easy, can it?" Aron opened the file, copied the code and dropped it onto the mining colony mainframe's terminal window.

The screen cleared.

> WELCOME TO MINING COLONY G646.

> ENTER SECONDARY AUTHORIZATION.

The cursor blinked, waiting for further input.

Aron shrugged. "What the heck." He dropped the next chunk of code from the file into the terminal window.

> CONNECTION ESTABLISHED.

Aron entered several commands into the terminal. Within seconds, the entire lunar colony system status results came up. After a few more commands, Aron snickered.

All around them, the *Artemis* main sensor displays lit up, with the colony structure's internal schematics coming alive on the screens. Various colored icons popped up, indicating locations of biological entities as well as heat sources and power signatures.

A triumphant grin spread across Aron's face. "Got 'em."

* * * *

"*Ten meters ahead, to the right,*" Aron Adler's voice announced over the comm. "*Be careful at this door. There are four sentries on the other side.*"

"Fuck," Kane murmured. "Can you do something about these damn strobe lights?"

"*Main power is down, but I'm turning on emergency lights. How's that?*"

The visual strobe alarms abruptly ceased. In their place, the overhead emergency lights activated. Each doorway was now dimly lit with a pale red light, as were the hallway intersections.

"Better, Aron."

"*Let me know when you're ready, Kane.*"

The strike team stopped at the metal doors that led to the inner biosphere of the mining colony. So far, they hadn't encountered any resistance. Now that Aron had hacked into the mining colony mainframe, they were able to get a complete sensor reading of the entire facility.

They'd been briefed on the sentries encountered by the *Cassini* crew. Weapons had been upgraded. Hopefully casualties would be nil.

The strike team got into position, but two of the Degans took point, aiming their pulse cannons, which shot pulses of high-energy particles more powerful than the standard Union rifles the rest of the party had. Beshel studied the cannons, immediately noting subtle changes in the design of the massive weapon that were unfamiliar. Apparently, the Degan Armed Forces had recently received upgraded combat armaments.

Once everyone was ready, Robertson activated his comm. "On my mark, Aron. Three… two… one… mark."

The door let out an echoing metallic *clang*. The sound of grinding gears and metal replaced it as the doors began to slide apart.

As soon as there was enough space, one of the eight-foot tall sentry cyborgs stepped through. The two slotted eyes on its dome-shaped head glowed bright red. It lifted its arms and fired the particle weapons built into its metal structure. The first beam went straight through Private Samuels, bisecting him at the chest. He crumpled to the ground, dead before he even knew what hit him.

Kane shouted and began to fire.

The phase cannons and Degan weapons brought the sentry down, but before they could regroup, three more came through the door, splitting weapons fire between them.

"Aim for the neck," Robertson shouted.

Lieutenant Elbar let out a roar, advanced, and fired. The particle beam flashed a brilliant orange as it exploded from the cannon. The crackling ball of energy hit one of the sentries in the joint under its head. The sound of metal shearing echoed throughout the chamber as sparks and metal fragments rained down from the robot's gaping wound. A second shot rendered the sentry completely inoperative.

The other Degans dispatched the other two sentries similarly.

Slinging his rifle over his shoulder, Elbar looked smug. "Got any more you need taken care of?"

Robertson looked impressed. "I need to get me one of those." He activated his comm. "Aron? What can you see?"

"We've got two dozen human lifesigns in what looks like the main lab area."

"Are they mobile?"

"No. It looks like they're holed up. I'm assuming they're protecting their research. They're cut off from the landing platform."

"Any non-humans?"

"I'm picking up one Degan lifesign down the left corridor, last room."

"That must be Lieutenant Drago."

"Degans don't have embedded ID chips, so I can't be certain who's who, but it stands to reason..."

Beshel followed Robertson and Durant down the corridor.

Using their lights to guide the way, they made their way to the end of the corridor without resistance.

Robertson pointed his flashlight at the heavy metal door. He read the fading stenciled print. "Ore Processing 1." When he popped the door control with his fist, it barked a denial. "Aron? Can you override the door?"

"*Done.*"

The door control beeped and the magnetic lock disengaged. Robertson kicked it open with his boot, then entered, rifle aimed and ready.

Beshel followed, moving around Robertson's big frame to get a look at the room.

An industrial grade conveyor belt system bisected the two-story room. Located overhead, it moved at a snail's pace, rolling toward a large furnace located deeper in the complex. Though the furnace was beyond the walls of this room, the intense heat and bright yellow-orange light spilled into the room from the conveyor opening.

Beshel reached up and wiped the beads of sweat beginning to form on his forehead.

"Oh my god," Robertson's young lieutenant shouted in horror.

Beshel swung around toward Lieutenant Yates's voice, hitting the blue-eyed kid with his flashlight. He then moved his light to where Yates was looking.

A pile of corpses sat in a shallow bin next to a massive mechanical arm. Given the pinching scoopers on the end of the arm, its function was presumably to take the items from the bin and place them onto the moving conveyor belt for meltdown.

Frozen in place, Beshel swallowed the bile that had risen in his throat as he scanned the pile with his flashlight.

As he searched for faces among the tangled limbs, the robotic arm came to life, its scoopers snatching one of the corpses. The body's head rolled back as it was lifted into the air.

The light from Beshel's flashlight illuminated the face of a young Degan male. Lifeless eyes stared back at Beshel.

He rushed forward. "Martan!"

Chapter 22

Beshel struggled to free the young Degan from the robotic arm, but he was caught tight in the jaws of the scoop's pincers.

"Get back, Chief." Durant blasted the appendage's joints, shearing it and sending the scooper assembly to the floor with a loud *bang*.

As soon as it was on the ground, Yates and the *Cassini*'s medic joined Beshel in pulling Martan to the side. Squatting next to the body, Beshel trained his flashlight on the young Degan's face.

It was not Martan.

"This isn't Martan. It's not my nephew." While part of Beshel was relieved, at the same time, part of him was horrified. Whoever this was, he was barely of age. Had he been reported missing? Did he have a family worried sick about him?

"Jesus," Yates whispered, his voice quivering. He tugged at the tattered white cotton top that covered the Degan's upper body. Well, at one time it was white. Now it was filthy—smeared with dried blood and dirt. Stenciled on the front of the top was the marking "D7".

"Goddamn it," Robertson cursed.

"D7…" Beshel knew what that designation meant. The scientists had labeled *him* as "Subject D2" in their data files. He fell back on his haunches and wanted to weep. Would he find "D3" through "D6" among these bodies? Would Martan be among these bodies? His voice croaked. "We need to check the other bodies."

Robertson stepped away, but Beshel could still hear him. "Aron? We've got bodies down here. I'm going to have Yates collect DNA samples so we can identify them, and notify their families."

"*Yes, sir,*" came the somber reply.

Beshel's hands shook as he checked the other bodies. There was no sign of Martan, but they found other "D" subjects, the highest number being D9.

Durant placed a hand on Beshel's shoulder. "You okay, Chief?"

"Yes. I really need to find my nephew. I'll never forgive myself if he ends up like this."

"We'll find him, Chief." Durant lowered his voice. "And we'll make all of them pay for what they've done."

"We're still picking up one Degan lifesign in the room that's not a member of the strike team. There's got to be someone else there."

Following Aron's lead, Beshel, and Durant and his men maneuvered through the processing room. They found another robotic arm platform in the far corner. Martan lay unconscious on the platform. He was stripped naked. The two spider-bots used the implements on their arm to poke and prod his nephew.

"Medic!" Beshel shouted.

He aimed his rifle and fired, hitting one of the bots head on. A second shot demolished it as Durant did the same with the other.

"I need a medic!"

* * * *

Peri raced down the corridor toward the shuttle bay, following Kenji and Aron. Because Aron was working with the sensors and Peri's baby, they decided to bring Martan aboard the *Artemis* for treatment. Aron knew more about Degan physiology and was more familiar with the scientists' methods.

The *Cassini* chief medical officer, Doctor Moore, had gone down to the surface with a security team to retrieve Martan.

Once the bay repressurized, the shuttle doors opened. Dr. Moore hurried down the ramp, followed by two security officers carrying an unconscious Martan on a stretcher. Another officer carried a closed crate. "We brought the remains of two bots for analysis."

"I did an initial assessment on Martan in the field," Dr. Moore said as they rushed to the medical bay. "He has a deep puncture wound in his hip, a particle burn on his chest, and an abrasion around his left ankle."

Peri was worried. Devin and his family loved Martan. If something happened to him, they would be devastated. And it would be Peri's fault. Martan wouldn't be here if he hadn't volunteered to help Peri on the mission.

He glanced over at Kenji, who had been quiet the entire time. He just stared straight ahead, completely silent.

After they reached the medical bay, Peri and Kenji hung back and let the doctors work.

"Has he been unconscious the entire time?" Aron asked.

"Yes," Dr. Moore replied as she ran a med scanner up and down Martan's body several times. "When the strike team found him, he was already unconscious." She read the data on her screen. "He's been given a massive dose of the sedative hexazolam."

Aron ran his own scans. "Even with Degan physiology, we need to make sure his heart and respiratory rates don't drop too low."

"Agreed." She placed a mask over Martan's nose and mouth and tapped a few controls on the bed's overhead monitor. After studying the screen for a moment. "Hypopnea leveling out."

While Dr. Moore concentrated on Martan's chest injury, Aron worked the wound on his hip. "They were attempting to harvest marrow and stem cells from the iliac crest."

Dr. Moore glanced back at Kenji and Peri. She turned back to Aron and lowered her voice. "According to Robertson and Durant, they were also attempting to harvest his reproductive cells."

Peri wanted to be sick. He knew exactly what they would try to do with those cells. And he also knew if Beshel was captured, they would drill into him and torture him until they'd harvested every bit of genetic material they could get out of him.

Kenji placed a hand on Peri's arm and handed him a glass of water. "Here. You won't do anyone any good if you pass out." Kenji watched the doctors for a few moments more, before muttering softly, "Martan will be fine. You'll see. He's strong."

Peri knew Kenji was probably right. While still worried about

Martan, Peri had to admit he was even more worried about the sire of his child.

After letting out a deep breath, Kenji picked up the crate left by the security officer. Putting it onto one of the science exam stations, he opened it up. He let out a startled grunt and shuddered. "Holy..."

"What is it?" Peri asked.

He peered over Kenji's shoulder to find the remnants of a metal object sitting in a pool of blackish-purple goo. Metallic limbs, wires, and fragments filled the box. A curved chunk of dark titanium sat on top of the mess. To Peri's horror, it contained an organic eye, built in as if it was a part of it. Though it was dead, it seemed as if it stared back at Peri.

With a startled gasp, Peri dropped the glass in his hand. The acrylic bounced on the floor, spraying water all over Peri's legs.

"That's Besh's eye."

* * * *

"Aron?" Robertson repeated the call into his comm mic. "Come in."

"Sergeant? This is Lieutenant Kanataka. Aron isn't available right now. He's busy with Lieutenant Drago."

Robertson glanced over at Beshel. "How is the lieutenant?"

"He's going to be fine. Aron and the doctors are patching him up. Once the sedative wears off, Dr. Moore says he should wake on his own."

Beshel let out a sharp breath. He gave a nod of appreciation to Robertson.

With Aron busy taking care of Martan, it was Lieutenant Kanataka who was now guiding them through the complex. *"Go back the way you came,"* Kenji ordered through the comm link. *"Make a left. You'll need to go up one level, find the heavy blast doors marked 'A01'. That's the entrance to admin."*

Durant pointed toward the second story, the wall opposite the conveyor that led to the furnace. A bank of windows overlooked the processing room. The blinds were drawn, blocking visual inspection.

Just as Beshel was about to turn away, something out of the corner of his eye caught his attention. Movement. A shadowed silhouette had stepped back from the window.

"There's someone up there."

"Team," Robertson barked. "Move out."

Following Kenji's directions, they made their way back to the blast doors.

"The bulk of facility administration is behind this door. Offices, security, technology. The main control room is at the far end, and it overlooks ore processing."

Beshel shot Robertson a look. "That's where they're holed up."

"Can you override the door controls?" Robertson asked.

"I'm on it."

The men fanned out in attack formation, weapons drawn and ready. Once Robertson got the acknowledgement from Durant and Elbar, he let Kenji know. "We're a go, Lieutenant. Open the door."

"Yes, sir."

With a loud thud, the metal doors began to move, slowly sliding apart. Beshel shifted to the left a step, trying to peer inside. Before he could get a gauge on what was beyond the doors, they came to a halt and started to slide closed.

"Kenji, override the door control!" Robertson commanded.

The door mechanism slowed. The controls inside sounded as if they were fighting with each other, wanting to open and close at the same time. Sounds of shearing metal echoed through the vaulted chamber.

Beshel recognized the familiar whirring sound as the first spider-bot appeared in the door crack. Hovering at the top of the opening, its particle weapon appendage lifted and aimed.

"Fire!" Durant shouted.

Beshel stepped back and aimed his rifle toward the ceiling. "Elbar! Don't let them touch you!"

Besh blasted the bot and it fell to the floor with a clang in front of his feet. The abomination's soulless eyes stared back at Beshel. *Like staring into your own death.* He kicked the still moving piece of shit, then fired a close range blast to destroy it. Black goop splattered against his boot.

The bot was followed by another. And another. Then another, coming faster and faster. In an endless wave, they poured out of the door crack, shooting webs, firing their weapons.

There were so many of them, Beshel lost count. He fired over and over, but for every one he destroyed, another two took its place.

The man in front of Beshel went down with a shout that was immediately silenced.

"*Artemis*," Beshel shouted into his comm. "We're being overrun with spider-bots!"

* * * *

"Do something!" Peri cried.

"Uh…" Kenji was flustered. "God damn it, I'm a geneticist, not a freaking spider-bot hacker." The sensor display showed the location of the strike team inside the complex. Their yellow icons were being pushed back by a never-ending swarm of red dots.

Peri looked at Kenji, who stood mouth agape, white as a ghost. "What are you going to do?"

Kenji opened his mouth, then closed it. "I have no idea."

"Well, you better come up with one. You got a box of spiders right here. Figure it out!"

Kenji pursed his lips and shot Peri a scathing look. He turned back to the box of parts and began pulling the pieces out. "Gross," he spat. He grabbed an air compressor and a portable vac. After cleaning it, he gave it a brief inspection then tossed it down on the exam table. "Worthless."

Aron joined Kenji at the table. "Martan is stable now. Doctor Moore is patching him up. What do we got here?" He picked up a fragment containing an eye. "Oh god, this is just so wrong."

"Tell me about it." Peri frowned as a cold shiver shot down his spine.

Kenji held up a metal fragment. Bolted to the inside was a shielded box, still coated in dark goop. "I think this might be the control node," he said with cautious excitement in his voice. He glanced around, holding his goopy hand in the air. With an annoyed sigh, he wiped away the goo on his uniform. He used a screwdriver to remove the metal shielding. Inside was a green circuit board that contained various chips.

Aron peered over Kenji's shoulders. "That looks like standard off-the-shelf system on a chip. It even has a universal service port."

"What good does that do?" Peri asked.

Kenji had extracted the circuit board from the fragment. He flipped it around, looking at the front and back. "We can download its command system."

Aron had already snagged a cable and connected it to the *Artemis* lab system. "That's what I was thinking." He handed Kenji the other end of the cable.

Kenji sighed and shrugged. "It's worth a shot."

Peri looked at the scientists with skepticism. "Yeah, well, I just hope you don't turn the entire ship into a giant spider-bot."

"Connection established," Aron said, ignoring Peri's comment. "Yeah, it's a standard SOC. They didn't even encrypt the firmware."

Aron and Kenji snickered.

Peri didn't really get the joke, and he sure didn't understand the code that was scrolling its way down the computer screen. He could only hope they knew what the hell they were doing, because Beshel was fast running out of time.

* * * *

"Captain Teldo to Lieutenant Elbar."

The Degan Lieutenant Elbar shot one of the bots with his cannon, obliterating it. "Go, Captain."

"Fall back. Return to the shuttle."

"Captain?" Elbar exchanged a look with Beshel.

"Return to the ship immediately. You have sixty minutes until we detonate

the facility from orbit."

"Yes, sir. Degan strike team, pull back!"

Beshel and the others were too busy trying to fight off the spider bots to convince Elbar and his team to stay. They were already retreating back from the blast doors. Tactically, it made sense. The place was overrun with these fucking bots. They couldn't risk anyone escaping. If they could destroy the facility and the men inside, they could stop these scientists for good.

Unfortunately, Beshel was still stuck here. Not to mention the Union officers.

"Damn cowards," Durant murmured. Beshel glanced over at the large human, who had slid up to his side. "We're fucking pinned down here."

Another man let out a pained scream in the distance as more bots came through the door.

"Corporal!" Yates called out. "Look out!"

Beshel felt the heat of a particle ray blast past his face as he swerved to the right.

"Fuck!" Durant screamed as he dropped to his knees. His rifle clattered to the floor. Blood poured from the smoldering hole in his armor, where his right arm met his shoulder. The smell of burning flesh permeated the air. The way his arm hung limp at his side, Beshel was sure the man would need months of rehab after surgery—provided they didn't have to amputate.

Beshel moved in front of Durant, shielding the fallen officer. He aimed his weapon and destroyed the bot that had shot the human. Another took its place. Everywhere he turned, the goddamned spiders were there. He was completely surrounded.

The bot lowered its weapon and raised its web arm, pointing it directly at Beshel.

* * * *

"Bragman to med bay."

Kenji stood up straight, as if Captain Bragman himself was in the room. "Go ahead, Captain."

"Captain Teldo is preparing to nuke the mining facility. We've got less than sixty minutes to evacuate our people and round up the rogues. If there's anything you can do to help our teams out, now would be the time."

"Right, Captain. We're on it."

"Keep me informed. Bragman out."

"What about the weapon systems?" Kenji asked.

Aron shook his head in frustration. "No. We can't reprogram the weapon systems over the air." His voice rose in volume. "They're embedded in the firmware, and we don't have time to debug their custom spaghetti code in sixty minutes." He slammed his fist on the table.

Peri looked at the clock. "Actually, we're talking like thirty minutes if we want to give them time to get back."

"You're not helping," Aron snapped.

Kenji reached out and squeezed his friend's hand. "Kane will be okay, Aron. You'll see."

Aron smiled mirthlessly. He opened his mouth to say something, but instead he gasped. "Wait. We don't have time to go through *their* code, but we know the standard firmware's commands. We have the documentation."

"Yes!" Kenji nodded in agreement. "We just have to find the right command."

Aron and Kenji scrolled through the processor's interface documentation, both desperately searching for the "right command".

Peri sat at one of the terminals and flipped through the documentation as well, but he didn't really know what he was looking for. "What about the 'Power Down' command?" he asked. It seemed obvious to him.

Aron shook his head. "No. That command is protected. We need to be *local* to access it; we can't do it remotely."

"Okay." Peri swiped to the next page. "What about the 'Recharge' command?"

Again Aron shook his head. "No. That command's also—

Wait. We can't tell them to *recharge*. But maybe we can trick them into thinking that they *need* to recharge."

Peri blinked. "Huh? Isn't that the same thing?"

"Not quite. Find the configuration settings."

He and Kenji frantically tapped at their screens.

"Here it is," Kenji said, showing his screen to Aron.

Reading off Kenji's screen, Aron brought up the configuration profile. Fingers moving swiftly, he tapped on the "Battery Module" icon and changed the chip's part number. "I'm changing the battery and cascading the mod throughout the network. This should trick the bots into thinking they have new batteries, which should automatically trigger a recharge command." He drew in a deep breath. "Here goes nothing."

Peri held his own breath as Aron pressed a final button on his screen.

* * * *

Corporal Durant groaned through gritted teeth. His arm hung limp at his side, but he strained to reach the rifle on the ground with his good hand.

"Save your strength, Corporal," Beshel said.

"I'm not going down without a fight."

With a couple dozen bots surrounding them, there wouldn't be much of a fight. Beshel looked around and found the other surviving strike team members in the same boat, including Sergeant Robertson and the young blond lieutenant.

Robertson tapped the commlink in his ear. "Aron," he whispered hoarsely. "I love you."

The man's pain echoed in Beshel's chest. The image of Peri's face floated up from his memory. Beshel watched Robertson's hand tighten on his rifle, his finger on the trigger, ready.

They exchanged a glance, and each nodded. This was their last stand, and they would go down fighting. No way in hell would Beshel end up like those poor men in the ore processing room, discarded like trash once the scientists were done torturing them.

A blue laser scanner flashed down Beshel's body. His muscles tightened as he readied to spring into action. As soon as the scanning bot lifted its web arm, he would make sure it would be nothing more than a splatter of purple goo.

The bot lowered its scanner arm, then paused. Several lights blinked, and it momentarily dropped down several inches before slowly rising back up to its previous level, as if its hover control was having issues.

Before Beshel could fully process what was going on, it turned a one-eighty and disappeared through the blast doors, back into the administration wing. One by one, the rest of the bots followed.

"What the fuck?"

Beshel looked at Robertson, who stood his ground with a proud smirk on his face. "That's my baby." Lifting his rifle, he looked around at the rest of the men. "Let's go."

The mining facility's administration wing had been retrofitted into a modern laboratory. Dozens of leading-edge computer workstations were surrounded by high-tech lab spaces. Various biological and technological experiments met in an unholy alliance. Cubby holes lined one wall, each filled several spider bots deep.

Men in white lab coats scrambled around. "They're all offline," one cried as he plugged a cable into one of the inactive bots.

Another shouted from a workstation, "They hacked our network!"

"Shut it down!"

Beshel fired his rifle, hitting the computer station before the asshole could shut anything down. It exploded in a shower of fire. The scientist screamed, covering his face with his hands as he fell backward. One of his comrades rushed to his aid, stamping out the fire with his lab coat.

"Stay right where you are!" Beshel shouted. "By order of the Degan Federation Bureau of Investigation and Galactic Planetary Union Security, this facility is shut down, and you are all under arrest."

There was movement from the corner of his eye, but before Beshel could turn, a particle beam blasted one of the scientists, and he crumpled to the floor in a dead heap.

"Anyone else wanna be a hero?" Robertson sneered. His men moved into strategic positions.

Beshel motioned with his rifle. "All of you move against that wall."

Robertson gave Yates a look. With a nod of his head, Yates extracted plastic ties from one of his uniform's utility pockets. One by one, he secured the criminals' hands behind their backs.

"Robertson to *Cassini*. We're in admin. We've taken control of the facility."

The last of the scientists to be cuffed made a break. As he separated from the group, Beshel recognized the man. With red hair and eyeglasses, his sniveling face was permanently etched in Beshel's now reclaimed memories of that night back on Earth.

"*You*," Beshel snarled. "You violated me and my—"

'Red' moved with his back along the wall of computer monitors. "You can't stop the Earth Liberation Movement. It has already begun. What we started will only spread."

Beshel seethed. His finger rubbed against his rifle's trigger. He hadn't asked to be part of this lunatic's "movement." With a simple squeeze, justice would be served for him, Peri and the offspring—not to mention the young Degans they'd tortured.

"We need him alive, Chief Drago."

Beshel ground his teeth together, resisting the urge to glare at Robertson. He didn't need a human telling him his job.

Taking advantage of the distraction, Red ducked down, pulling something from underneath one of the workstations. He cupped a portable gas mask over his mouth as he ran across the room toward a Plexiglas-encased button on the wall. Just as he flipped open the cover, Beshel fired his weapon.

The scientist shrieked as he pulled back a smoldering stump. Gripping his severed wrist, he dropped to his knees, a sobbing mess.

The smell of burning flesh and blood permeated the air.

Beshel crinkled his nose, disgusted by both the smell and the human. "I told you to stay where you were." He turned back to Robertson, who looked quite impressed. "Don't worry, he'll live. Now get him out the fuck of my sight."

Chapter 23

After making sure the injured Durant was strapped in, Beshel jabbed him with a field medic sedative pack. Hurriedly, he returned to the cockpit and buckled himself into the co-pilot's seat. He watched from the shuttle's viewport as the spacecraft lifted off, heading back to the *Artemis*. The mining colony grew smaller and smaller as they picked up speed and distance.

The shuttle's comm system came alive with a ping. The captain of the Degan battleship *Akbal*'s voice echoed through the cabin. *"Brace for impact, on my mark. Three. Two. One. Mark."*

A second later, the moon caved in on itself, then exploded in a brilliant ball of light. He wanted to witness the destruction—to verify the research station and all of its wicked secrets were gone once and for all—but eventually the brilliance became too much. Beshel closed his eyes and turned away from the window.

The shuttle lurched as the shockwave hit it, but the turbulence quickly ended.

Only then did Beshel open his eyes.

When he looked where the lunar outpost should have been, he saw nothing but a crater underneath a cloud of dust and debris.

It was over.

* * * *

Beshel read through the data on his comPad once more. The men dressed in the Union uniforms, the ones who had bombed the Degan Institute and stolen his child, were known mercenaries. With this information, they'd be able to trace back the money trail.

As for the incriminating evidence against Aron… that didn't need any more digging. He knew exactly who planted it, and he was pretty sure he knew why. Again, he needed to look no further than the money trail.

It all seemed to come back to money, didn't it?

After transmitting his findings to Agent Barlan, Beshel headed straight for sickbay.

As soon as he entered, he found Martan laid out on one of the biobeds. A blushing Kenji hovered over him. They both whispered softly to each other. When they realized Beshel had walked into the room, Kenji stepped back and tried to look professional.

"Nephew, I'm glad to see you alive and well."

"Thanks, Uncle. It's just a burn and some minor cuts."

"I trust you're in good hands here?"

"The best." Martan smiled at Kenji.

Kenji returned the smile. He glanced at Beshel, then quickly turned away, pretending to monitor the readings on the display above the bed.

Martan slid his hand to the edge of his mattress, where it came into the slightest of contact with the outside of Kenji's leg. Beshel noticed that young human scientist did not move away from the covert touch, nor did he acknowledge it.

"I'm fine too, by the way," Durant shouted from across the room.

Laughing, Beshel moved to Durant's bedside. The Marine's right arm was wrapped in heavy bandages, immobilized inside a sling taped to his chest. "I got a round of surgeries when we get back to starbase, but I'll be fine. I've had worse."

Durant held out his left hand.

Beshel took it, and the two men shared a long handshake. "Good work, Corporal."

"You too, Agent."

After checking in with the rest of the casualties, Beshel found Peri in the back corner of the lab, hovering over the incubator unit. Dr. Adler performed scans on the unit, double-checking the readings before entering data into one of the lab's workstations.

Peri stroked his fingers across the glass. "Aron says it's time to move him to the maturation chamber."

"I can't believe how much he's grown."

"I know... We just got him back yesterday..."

Aron and Kenji returned, now wearing sterile aprons and gloves.

"We're ready to move the baby," Aron said. "The phase II maturation unit will supply nutrients, and regulate the baby's temperature and air mixture as he continues to develop for the next couple of weeks. Now, the transition from a liquid to air environment might look traumatic, but I assure you, everything will be okay."

Peri and Beshel both nodded automatically.

Beshel was pretty sure Peri really couldn't handle "traumatic" right now, so he just hoped what Aron was telling them was the truth. Beshel moved up behind Peri and wrapped his arms around him, wanting to comfort and calm him. Automatically, Peri leaned back into Beshel's body, and it greatly pleased Beshel.

A smile spread across Beshel's face and he let out a soft breath. He hadn't anticipated that Peri's presence would be comforting to him as well. As he held the human, he stroked his thumb back and forth across Peri's ribs, and nuzzled his nose against the top of Peri's head.

While Kenji prepared the maturation unit, Aron worked on the incubator. When the liquid had drained out, the baby boy squirmed and coughed, the noise sounding tiny and frail.

Peri held his breath.

Reaching into the incubator, Aron used a small device to clear the baby's mouth and nose while he gently rubbed a pair of fingers against the middle of his chest. After a few seconds, the boy's breathing evened out. "There you go, little one..." He turned toward Peri and Beshel. "See? He's fine."

At the same time, Peri's finally exhaled. "Thank you."

After cleaning him completely of the pink gel, Aron pulled out the delicate baby, cupped in the palm of his hands. He turned toward the maturation chamber, but stopped and looked back at Beshel.

"Would you like to hold him?" he asked.

Beshel started and his body went rigid. "What?"

"Just for a moment."

Letting go of Peri and stepping backward, Beshel shook his head strongly. "Let Peri hold him."

Aron exchanged a look with Peri. He turned back to Beshel, and indicated a box of sterile gloves with a tilt of his head. "Grab a pair. Don't worry. They'll stretch to fit."

Reluctantly, Besh pulled a pair of gloves from the box. No sooner had he managed to get them on his hands than Aron placed the babe in his cupped palms.

"Wait. I don't know what to do. What if I…"

Beshel's voice trailed off. He couldn't pull his eyes away from his sleeping son. He was warm in his palms, and his tiny chest rose and fell as he struggled to breathe the ship's air on his own. Fine wisps of dark hair covered the crown of his head.

He could see Peri's soft human features in his face, but he could also tell he'd have the strong, sturdy build of a Degan male.

He was beautiful.

As Beshel memorized every millimeter of the child's face, his eyes caught a barely visible mark on his left earlobe. A tiny *heart*.

The baby hiccupped, and Beshel drew in a concerned breath. Within seconds, the boy began to breathe steadily again.

A tear fell from his eye, and landed on his boy's head. Using his thumb, Beshel swiped it away. The black hair was fine as down against the pad of his thumb. He hadn't known the child for more than a few minutes and already knew he loved him. Deep down in his soul, he knew this babe was a part of him. Beshel would do anything in his power to protect him.

At the same time, he realized those feelings weren't just for the baby.

And he'd been wrong. So very wrong.

Beshel lifted his head and sought out Peri. Another tear fell from his eye. His voice caught. He spoke softly, not wanting the entire medical bay to know how close he was to losing his emotional control. "Forgive me, Peri."

Peri wiped at his own eyes. "For what, Besh?"

"For denying our son. For denying you... my bondmate."

* * * *

Peri shut the door to their quarters and hit the *lock* control. His heart was about to beat right out of his chest, and had been ever since Beshel dropped that bomb on him.

"Bondmate?"

Beshel stared at the floor, but nodded his head. "Yes."

"I thought you didn't believe in that? Why do you now?"

"I didn't want to believe it. I didn't want to think about it. But after holding our boy..." Beshel shook his head back and forth. "After we made love... There's no other explanation."

"But we didn't, you know..."

Beshel cringed, and looked up and met Peri's eyes. "We did. Our first time. I pulled out, remember?"

"Yeah. I remember Old Faithful erupting on me, but I don't remember any locking."

"Old Faithful?"

"Never mind that. Keep going."

"For about twenty minutes after I pulled out, my erection was swollen. I was still coming, leaking semen. Fuck, it hurt." Beshel shuddered. "You were asleep, but the urge to pin you down and shove it back inside you— It was nearly uncontrollable."

"All righty then. I get the picture."

"And there were the pheromones. When we made love, my body released the mating scent."

"Yeah." The memory of that scent was enough to make Peri's dick move in his pants. "I remember."

"I should have told you. It was wrong of me to deny you." Beshel turned his head as his eyes pressed shut. "I was wrong. It was disgraceful. It was without honor."

Peri closed the distance between them. "You *were* wrong for not telling me. But you're telling me now. And I forgive you, Besh. And maybe you lied to yourself, and to me, but you're not without honor. You're the most honorable man I know."

Beshel opened his eyes and stared Peri down. "I... I have feelings for you."

The words weren't exactly romantic. Knowing Besh, that was as about an undying commitment of love as he was going to get right now. But the feeling in the words and the sincerity on Besh's face were enough to do Peri in.

"I love you, too," he confessed.

Peri pressed up onto his tiptoes and pulled Besh down for a kiss. Sweet and tender quickly escalated to steamy and torrid. Besh's tongue was insistent, invading Peri's mouth, plundering it. Peri pushed his tongue forward, trying to keep up with Besh, tangling them together. He felt the flat fronts of Beshel's lower canine teeth pressing against his chin and lower lip. It was a strange sensation, but it was hot.

Beshel made as if he was going to pull back, but he kept kissing Peri's lips. Finally he tilted his head back. "If we do this now, I don't know if I'll be able to stop this time."

"I don't want you to stop." Peri grabbed Beshel's head and pulled it down for another kiss, but Beshel stopped him.

"If we do this, it will be permanent."

"I understand."

"You're my bondmate, Peri." The words were said with conviction.

Beshel's voice and the look in his eyes were almost enough to make Peri lose it. No one had ever in his life looked at him that way. He'd been waiting for this moment for as long as he could remember. There would be no turning back. Peri could only nod his response. He didn't want to start crying.

Beshel lowered Peri to the bed. As he removed Peri's clothes, he touched and kissed every exposed inch of skin. Goosebumps erupted all over Peri's body. He trembled as Beshel's mouth and fingers ramped up his need.

Once he was naked, Peri helped Besh pull off his uniform, tossing it onto the floor with the rest of their clothes.

Besh was on top of Peri, between his wide-spread legs. Peri pulled his knees toward his chest, and canted his hips up, giving Besh easier access.

This time it would be face to face.

Taking his time, Besh kissed up and down Peri's neck. He moved down to Peri's chest.

"I don't understand whey you have these," Besh muttered to himself.

Peri assumed it was a rhetorical question. Besh attacked his right nipple with his mouth, sucking hard while flicking his tongue back and forth across the rapidly hardening nub. While pleasuring the right nipple, Besh used his fingers to tweak the left one. Peri's response was to arch his back and cry out in pleasure.

The Degan was clearly fascinated with his nipples. Peri moved his hands to Besh's head, encouraging him to continue. Each lick and suck sent shivers down Peri's spine. His cock was harder than it had ever been—leaking and dripping pre-cum on his belly.

While he worked Peri's nipples, Besh's fingers found their way between his legs. Peri could only spread his legs and take it. Beshel's mouth assaulted his nipples while his fingers fucked his ass.

Everything Besh did to him sent Peri closer and closer to the edge. The pressure was building inside him, and he felt like he was on the verge of coming. Besh hadn't even touched his cock yet.

He loved how Besh took his time with him, making sure he was ready.

"Please, Besh."

Peri pressed his hips back against Besh's fingers, while he moved his hands back and forth across Besh's head. He dug his fingers into the larger man's fur, and when they came in contact with the horns, he leisurely stroked his fingers up and down the length.

A low growl burst from his throat as Besh's body jerked. *Oh, he liked that.* Peri would remember that for later, but right now he needed some dick.

"Please, Besh," he repeated while fluttering his fingers around the base of each horn.

Besh pulled away, adjusting his body so his cock was in position. He rubbed his cock up and down the crack of Peri's ass, spreading the secreted lube around and inside the hole. Peri felt the pressure of Besh's penetration, but he was ready for it. After a fleeting momentary pain, it subsided to a dull throb.

Peri looked up at Besh, who had his eyes closed tight. His jaw muscle twitched, and he let out a muted grunt. "Hard to... control..."

"I'm okay. You can move."

And Besh did. A thrust of his hips sent the engorged shaft deep into Peri's body. His balls slapped against Peri's ass. Peri drew in a sharp breath from the momentary bite of pain. But then Besh pulled back and thrust in again, jabbing his prostate on the way.

Peri let out the breath in a long moan.

Beshel thrust. Over and over, he thrashed Peri with abandon. While Besh held up his weight on his hands, Peri used his free hands to explore Besh's body. Underneath all that fur, his mate had a powerful physique. The strong corded muscles contracted with every movement.

"Your touch feels so good," Besh whispered hoarsely.

"You're so big and strong. I'm so glad I saved myself for you."

Beshel's eyes darkened as his pupils blew. "I will be the only one who's ever had you."

Peri smirked. His bondmate was turned on by his words, staking his territorial claim on Peri's body. "Yes," Peri encouraged. "The only one, ever."

Beshel doubled his efforts, pumping his cock in and out of Peri's ass. He snarled, showing off his teeth with a throaty growl. "Peri. I'm about to come."

Peri was right there with him. He arched his back off the bed, grinding his dick into the fur of Besh's torso. Just a little more friction was all he needed. "Don't stop, Besh. Don't stop."

Besh's breath came out in shallow pants as his rhythm caught. He sounded desperate. "I'm going to lock, Peri."

Oh wow. Okay.

Peri gripped the fur on Besh's back, fisting it so tight he was momentarily worried he was hurting his bondmate. His legs tightened, pressing against Besh's thighs. But then everything shattered, and he couldn't have cared less.

"Besh!"

The room began to spin as the first blast of semen shot from his body, splashing between them, the start of a sticky mess.

Even while in the throes of orgasm, Peri was aware of Besh roaring as his cock swelled inside him. It pulsed, growing and contracting, and Peri was filled with jets of hot liquid.

Besh let out a series of stuttered groans as his body shuddered repeatedly. His balance faltered, and he dropped heavily down on top of Peri. He struggled to right himself, but the backward movement made it feel like Besh was about to tear him in half.

Biting back a scream, Peri wrapped his arms around Besh, and pulled him back down. "It's okay. Let it go."

Beshel relaxed somewhat, but his body was still convulsing. The shockwaves rubbed against Peri's inner wall, sending pleasing waves of pressure against his prostate, and he let his eyes flutter closed.

They remained like this for several more minutes.

"This is kinda nice," he whispered. He now understood what Devin had said about the locking. It was a good thing he'd taken that pill. But… for the first time he wondered what it would be like to carry Beshel's baby the normal way. Not that there was anything *normal* about a human man getting pregnant.

"I thought for a moment you killed me," Besh said. "Death by orgasm. I felt like I left my body for a bit there."

"I can guarantee you never left *my* body."

"We're both going to be sore."

"I need a hot shower and a massage."

"When we get home, I'll arrange it."

When Beshel mentioned home, for the first time since leaving Earth, all Peri pictured was Dega.

* * * *

"Degan Shuttle 84656, you are cleared for take-off. U.S.C. Artemis *out."*

"Set course for home," Beshel said. He triple-checked that Peri and the maturation unit holding their son were safely strapped in before taking his own seat.

Martan tapped the comm control. "Thank you, *Artemis.*" He paused, looking out the window, lost in thought. With a shake of his head, he returned his attention to the control panel and took the shuttle out.

Once they cleared the *Artemis,* Beshel turned back to Martan. "Set course for home," he repeated.

When Martan didn't respond, Beshel reached over and touched his shoulder, causing his nephew to startle.

"Sorry, course laid in."

"Are you okay to pilot?"

"I'm fine."

Beshel chuckled. "I think you left your mind back on the *Artemis* with that human lieutenant."

Martan smiled. "I never met anyone like Kenji. He's so damn smart. And, mmm, he smells good."

Beshel exchanged a look with Peri, who rolled his eyes. "Hopefully you didn't leave him in a delicate state." Beshel laughed.

Martan frowned. *"Delicate?* What does that mean?"

Peri interjected. "He means he hopes you didn't knock him up." He patted his belly to make his point.

When it finally sunk in, Martan swung around in his chair, his mouth dropped open. "What?"

Peri chuckled. "Yeah, apparently the men in your family cause that peculiar mutation in human males."

Martan went pale. "You're not serious."

Peri shrugged. "Well, it's just a theory."

"It's not like we—" Martan stopped and glared at Peri and Besh. "You two are just fucking with me." Martan turned his attention back to his console, grumbling to himself.

Peri looked at Beshel and shrugged again.

Chapter 24

The starships *Artemis*, *Cassini*, and *Akbal* were all en route to Union Headquarters on Sargan III, their brigs full with prisoners who would be facing a long list of charges. They now had a name to go with their anti-Union crusade, the Earth Liberation Movement. The investigation would fall under Union jurisdiction. Beshel would let the humans and the other Union member worlds deal with whatever remained of that mess.

Presented with the evidence, Prime Minister Alden gave the order to the Degan Armed Forces to stand down. For now, war had been averted. Hopefully, the successful prosecution of the rogue humans would go a long way toward mending the relations between the Union and the Degans.

With this investigation finally nearing a close after nearly two long years, Beshel was looking forward to taking some leave and spending time at home. With Peri and the baby almost ready to come home soon, he had a family to build.

There was just one more loose end to tie up.

* * * *

As soon as they disembarked from the shuttle, they were greeted by Agent Barlan and the men on his A team. His brother Dashel was there, as well as his wife.

Beshel looked to his side, where Peri glanced around, looking unsure of himself.

Reaching out, Beshel took the human's hand and closed the distance between them.

The smirk on his older brother's face annoyed the fuck out of him, but he wasn't ashamed of Peri. And he wasn't ashamed to admit that he'd been wrong.

"Welcome home, brother." Dashel took Beshel in his arms and hugged him closely, giving him several hardy pats on the back.

Before Beshel let go, he softly said, "You were right, brother. About everything."

"I know." Dashel grinned and shot him a wink. "We'll talk more about that later." Turning away from Beshel, he moved to Peri. He stroked a hand over Peri's head, then tugged on the human's earlobe. "Welcome to the family, little brother."

Beshel cleared the lump in his throat as he watched his brother and sister-in-law shower Peri with warm greetings. An earlobe tug was a display of affection elders often used on young cubs. For Dashel to use it on his Peri was significant. Even though Peri likely didn't realize its meaning, it meant the world to Beshel.

Martan disembarked, and he was promptly scolded and praised simultaneously by his mother. When she saw him limping, you'd have thought the boy had actually lost a leg.

"Chief." Barlan handed Beshel a comPad. "We're standing by. A DAF military squad is ready to move in with us."

Beshel turned to Peri. "Go with Dashel. He'll make sure you get back to Bastian's okay."

"But…"

"I have one more thing I need to take care of, then this will be all over. I need you to make sure Martan is taken care of."

"Okay, but I have a feeling Nydia won't let Martan out of her sight for the next thirty years."

Beshel glanced toward his nephew. "You're probably right."

"Be careful, Besh."

Beshel cupped Peri's face in his hands and pressed a tender kiss to his lips. "I promise."

Minutes later, the investigators and the Degan Armed Forces squadron converged on the Degan Science Institute. Bypassing the security station, they went straight to the elevator banks. DSI security tried to stop them, but their credentials overrode their objections.

Beshel barged into Director Zorn's office.

The Director sat at his desk, frantically working at his computer.

"Don't bother, Zorn."

Zorn froze when he looked up and saw Beshel was flanked by four of Beshel's agents and six soldiers, all with weapons drawn.

"We've already executed the warrants on your financial records and your communication logs."

"How dare you!" Zorn huffed as he stood. "I am a federal director, appointed by the Prime Minister himself."

"You're under arrest, *Director*. For treason against the Federation, conspiracy to start war, inciting terror, bribery, and fraud. I seem to be forgetting a charge... Ah yes, the murder of Doctor Neolin Thorsel."

"You have no proof."

Beshel held up his pad. "We have the money transfers. Not only were you funding the xenophobes through your own personal bank account, but you took bribes from Grobel Consolidated—which amounts to a hefty bit of company stock—in exchange for weapons contracts. If the Degan Federation went to war, you would stand to become quite wealthy."

His eyes darted between the soldiers. "Those, uh, contracts were perfectly legal."

"We'll see. It was you that let the Earth Liberation Movement mercenaries into the lab, then sealed in Doctor Thorsel to keep your secret. You used the terror attack to urge the Prime Minister to go to war. I'm going to make sure you rot in prison for the rest of your life."

"But..." Zorn's eyes filled with tears and he choked back a sob. "I'm an appointed official," he whined. "I have friends..."

Beshel rolled his eyes. "Get this pathetic piece of shit out of my sight."

* * * *

"We still haven't given him a name yet."

Peri and Beshel sat in the U.S.C. *Artemis* medical lab, watching their son through the incubator window.

With all of the turmoil going on in the Degan Science Institute, they'd decided it would be best to let the baby remain on the *Artemis*. With tensions easing between their governments, the cruiser was allowed to remain docked at Degan Station until the baby was discharged into their care.

For the past three weeks, Peri and Besh had remained aboard the *Artemis*, and spent every free moment in the ship's medical bay. They watched the infant's chest rise up and down as he slept comfortably. It was obvious the boy had Degan DNA coursing through him. In the short time, he'd grown by leaps and bounds, and was now fully to term. He hadn't woken yet, but Dr. Adler assured them he would do so at any time. When he did, he would be ready to leave his "bubble."

In addition to his Degan physique, the boy had a healthy head of fine black hair. He got that from Peri, naturally. He had defined human facial features, but the rest of him looked Degan. Including the pair of nubs on top of his head that would grow into horns. Not to mention the tail that was curled up between his legs.

Beshel stroked his thumb across the incubator's glass, as if trying to make a physical connection to the boy. "I've given it some thought. How do you feel about Harikan?"

"Harikan? Harikan Drago. It sounds good. I like it."

"We could call him Hari."

Peri smiled. "Did you pick Hari because it rhymes with my name?"

"I didn't realize that until you said it aloud. Harikan means *miracle* in the Old Degan tongue."

Placing his hand on top of Beshel's, he gave it a squeeze. "I love it, Besh. It's perfect." He leaned into Beshel's body. "And I love you."

"I…" Besh coughed and cleared his throat. He swallowed audibly. "I love you, too."

Peri's disbelief was interrupted by the baby's muffled cough.

Beshel and Peri both sat up and leaned into the incubator to get a closer look.

Hari's dark eyelashes began to flutter. A couple of blinks, and Hari opened his eyes for the first time. His wide-open emerald green eyes moved around and finally focused on Peri and Besh.

As his son looked on him for the first time, Peri forgot how to breathe.

Beshel pressed his nose to the glass. "Oh my... look how beautiful you are."

"Hello, Hari." Peri gently tapped the glass, and Hari twitched. He blinked his big bright eyes and flexed his tiny, uncoordinated hands as he kicked his feet. Peri and Besh both giggled, overcome with joy.

When the chamber began to beep, Dr. Adler walked up and smiled. "Looks like someone's ready to meet his daddies."

This was the moment he'd been waiting for since this journey began, but Peri suddenly wished he'd had more time to get ready. But would he ever have had enough time to prepare for this?

Aron deactivated the chamber, and Hari began to cough. Then he began to wail bloody murder.

Peri panicked as he sat up straight in his seat. "Is something wrong?"

"He's just getting used to breathing outside of the regulated chamber." After a quick scan with his medical instrument, Aron tenderly wrapped Hari in a pastel yellow blanket. He placed the bundle in Peri's arms. "Say hello to..."

"Harikan," Peri finished.

"It's a beautiful name, for a beautiful boy. I'll be at my desk if you need me." With a touch of Peri's shoulder, Aron left.

"Look at him, Besh," Peri whispered, as if the volume of his voice might harm the baby.

"He's as beautiful as you are," Besh whispered back. "Why are we whispering?"

Peri kept whispering. "I don't know. But I think he likes it."

The two bondmates leaned down over their child, who simply stared back at them, mesmerized by the sight of his parents whispering to each other.

Chapter 25

Peri watched as Beshel removed Hari from the hovercar's baby seat. He wasn't worried, because Beshel was acting as if the baby was a nuclear device set to detonate at the slightest movement.

"You won't break him," he offered.

"I don't have as much practice as you do caring for babies."

"Yeah. Because *I'm* the expert," he said with a snort as he pulled his suitcase from the car.

"You know more than me." Beshel gingerly moved Hari into a cradling position, precisely—down to the millimeter—the way Dr. Adler had shown him. Peri would have to take advantage of Besh's OCD when it came to diaper changing. The man knew exactly how to do it.

Peri followed Beshel into the house. Standing at the front door, he looked around, suddenly feeling out of place. "Um... where should I put my stuff?"

"In my room— *Our* room." And now Beshel was self-conscious. "Unless you don't want to share a room, that is?"

"Do you?"

"I do...?" The word rose at the end, turning it into a question.

"It shouldn't be this awkward, should it? Are we making a mistake, rushing things?"

Beshel stopped and turned around, Hari cradled in his arms, giving Peri his full attention. "I don't feel like we're rushing things. But I feel we have a lot of catching up to do."

Peri nodded his agreement. "Yeah. When I left Earth, I certainly didn't expect to have a baby. I mean, you're supposed to get married first, right?" Peri snickered. "I mean, whatever are people going to think?"

Beshel frowned, concern written all over his face. "Does that bother you? That we haven't had a bonding ceremony?"

Peri held up a hand and took a step back. "Whoa. I was just joking. Let's not get ahead of ourselves."

Beshel shrugged. "Technically, we're bonded by law because of the whole *locking* thing. The ceremony is just a formality."

"I know…." Peri shuddered. Why in the world would they create laws around stuff like that? Didn't politicians have better things to do than butt into people's private lives? "Can't we just have some time just for us? You know, to get used to all of this. Before we tell everyone about the, uh, *locking*… and your brother's wife throws us one of her huge-ass parties."

Beshel chuckled. "We can only delay the inevitable for so long. Speaking of my brother, while we were on the *Artemis* waiting for Hari, he had your things brought over and had a room made up for Hari."

"I hope it's not over the top."

Beshel didn't answer; he just laughed.

Peri followed Beshel to the back of the house. He dropped his bag by Beshel's bedroom door, then went across the hall into the new nursery.

As soon as he entered the room, his jaw dropped. "Okay, I know I said 'no' to over the top, but this is just way over, and way perfect."

It was exactly the room Peri had dreamed of when he was growing up. His dreams never came true—no one wanted to adopt him, or to whisk him away to a fancy house with a fancy bedroom filled with everything a boy could want, like this one.

The room was painted a perfect shade of baby blue. Pristine white furniture filled the room, including an ornate crib fit for a prince. A mobile of baby animal figurines hung over the crib's head. The entire room was decorated with baby animals—Earth animals. They were so dang cute, Peri wanted to eat them all up.

Clearly Devin had a big hand in decorating this room.

"We can change it if you don't like it." Beshel moved close, enveloping an arm around Peri, pulling him in close.

Peri shook his head as his eyes welled with tears. His own dreams never came true... but Hari's would. Peri would spend every day of his life seeing to it.

* * * *

Standing by the floor length windows overlooking the back yard, Peri watched Besh and Hari play in the backyard.

Well, technically Besh was doing the playing, but Hari seemed happy. As Besh lifted him in the air and spun around in circles, Hari stared back at Besh with his big green eyes and a smile on his face. The baby boy always seemed to smile when he saw Besh or Peri—at least that was what Peri saw.

While his two men were occupied, Peri went to the fridge and pulled out some meat and cheese. As he set about fixing sandwiches, he couldn't help but smile, too. He and Hari had been living with Besh for over a week now. That initial awkwardness had quickly evaporated, and Peri thought of the lake house as his home now.

He joined them outside. After spreading a blanket on the grass, they sat down with Hari between them. Peri put the bottle of saki milk down in front of Besh as he began to fix their plates.

Beshel picked up the bottle. "Okay. First, test the temperature. Second..."

Peri laughed.

Once Hari finished his lunch, he fell asleep between Peri and Beshel, giving them time to enjoy their sandwiches at their own leisure.

The weather was beautiful once again, and the warm breeze carried the scent of the lake's blooming wildflowers through the air. The sun burned bright overhead, large and orange.

Peri closed his eyes for a few moments and breathed in the smells, letting the rays of the sun warm his face.

He looked down at his sleeping son. Peri didn't want to disturb him, but he was so adorable, Peri couldn't help but touch him. Ever so gently, he ran his fingers through the fine hair on top of his head, then rubbed the tip of an index finger across his little horns. Still unable to help himself, he tapped the tip of Hari's nose. "Boop."

Still the boy didn't wake.

When he looked up, Peri found Beshel watching him with a blissful grin on his face.

Feeling slightly exposed, Peri looked away, hoping he wasn't blushing like a fool. "How was your lunch?" he asked. He smoothed down Hari's onesie—the perfect powder blue one with the cartoon banti on it—and dabbed at a drop of milk that had spilled. He rubbed his wet finger on his shirt.

"It was perfect." Beshel leaned in, wiping his finger across Peri's bottom lip. "Sauce."

Peri smiled, his tongue peeking out to wipe away the remnants of said sauce. "Yeah. It was."

Of course, Peri wasn't talking about just the food. It was all of it. Being here with Besh and Hari, out under the warm sun, laying by the lake.

"I'm thinking we need a boat," Besh said. "Pontoon style. We could float around and relax on the water." Beshel waved his arm back and forth, making the motions of a boat floating along gentle waves.

"I've never been on a boat before, but it sounds nice...." Peri decided now was the time to bring up the subject he'd been fearing. "You won't get bored? Hanging out with me and Hari all day?"

"What do you mean?" Besh frowned.

"Twelve weeks is a long time away from work."

"Well, I earned the time off. I should get to use it."

"But you love your work."

"I do, but I have bigger priorities now. My family. Besides, when I go back, I'm going off active field duty."

Peri sat up, surprised at Besh's announcement. "What?"

"Agent Barlan is being promoted to Associate Chief. I'm assigning him to be in command of field operations. I'll be overseeing things from my office in the Capital."

"Really?"

"I'm the boss, remember? I can do whatever I want. So, I'll be home every night with you and the baby. I hope that's okay with you." He reached out and took Peri's hand.

Peri let out an exaggerated sigh. "I guess. I'll just have to deal with it."

Besh laughed. He pulled Peri close and pressed a soft kiss to Peri's lips. "I love you."

Chapter 26

There was something seriously wrong with Peri.

Watching Besh feed Hari and then bathe him shouldn't make him horny. But it did.

I'm a freak.

Peri reached down over his jeans and adjusted his erection. "You're such a good sire," he said from the bathroom doorway. God, why did that sound so slutty? Like something out of a porn clip.

Beshel tilted his head back and lifted a brow. "Are you feeling okay?"

"Oh, I'm fine, big boy."

Seriously? What was the matter with him?

Beshel just shook his head and laughed. Only Peri wasn't laughing. Was Besh secreting some more of those pheromones? Yes, that had to be it. God, Peri's body felt like it was on fire.

As soon as they got Hari into his crib and said their goodnights, Peri pulled Besh into their bedroom. He wasn't usually the one who initiated sex; he didn't need to. Beshel seemed to always want it, and was not the least bit shy about letting Peri know. But tonight, Peri just couldn't wait for him to come around and get things started.

"Nice kilt," he said as he dropped to his knees. Sliding his hands up Beshel's fur-covered trunk-like thighs, Peri went right for the goods. The custom of no underwear beneath the kilt was pretty damn convenient. He wrapped both of his hands around the thick shaft that hung flaccid, low and long between his mate's legs. It felt huge. It was as big as it was when hard, just as long, nearly as thick.

Lifting the front of the leather garment, Peri ducked his head under, taking the head of Beshel's cock into his mouth.

"Gods, Peri... Your mouth..."

Using both fists in concert with his mouth and tongue, it wasn't long at all before Besh was fully erect. The thick head tapped at the back of Peri's mouth, threatening to choke him. He could feel the rings beneath the skin of the shaft, pulsing and expanding. Enough pre-cum flowed that Peri was forced to swallow.

Beshel was ready.

Peri pulled back and unbuckled the kilt. As soon as it fell to the floor, he pushed Beshel backwards until the Degan fell back onto the bed.

Besh was already breathing hard, his eyes open wide as he stared back at Peri. His cock, thick and wet, stuck up into the air, pointing toward the head of the bed.

"Nice."

His body felt like it was on fire. He needed to be naked—right now. Peri tore off his clothes and pounced onto Besh, straddling his hips. Beshel's cock nestled into the crack of his ass, and Peri rolled his pelvis. He felt the heat of pre-cum as it oozed out and slicked between Peri's ass cheeks. Reaching behind him, Peri swirled his fist around Besh's shaft. His hand was nice and slippery when he pulled away. He lifted his hips slightly and pushed a finger inside. He replaced that finger with two. He closed his eyes as he stretched himself.

Besh growled. "You are so sexy, my mate."

They'd never done it in this position before, but Peri was eager to try it. The thought of having a little bit of control made him even hotter.

"What's going on with you today?" Beshel asked, before quickly adding, "Not that I'm complaining."

"I want you," Peri admitted. "I need your cock."

"Fuck. Then get it. Ride me." Beshel growled as his hands clamped each side of Peri's waist.

"Oh yeah," Peri breathed.

"Make me come. Make me lock inside you."

"Oh god." Peri quivered from the thought. That was exactly what he needed. Instinctually, he knew it was the only thing that would cure his need.

Lifting up, he reached between his legs and pulled back Beshel's cock. Guiding the naturally lubed head to his entrance, he lowered himself onto it. When the blunt head breached his body, Peri held his breath. As he took him in deeper, he exhaled with a moan. It stretched him wide, and felt so hot inside him. It was so warm, so wet, so slick.

Peri gripped Beshel's hands and began to move. Slowly and cautiously at first, he quickly became accustomed to the movements of this position. Instinctually, his body knew what to do. It knew what he needed.

He bounced up and down, riding Beshel hard and fast. The Degan's naturally secreted lubrication made it easy to take him.

"Yes," Besh growled. "Ride me. Gods, you smell so fucking good."

"So do you," Peri panted.

The sound of their harsh breathing and the wet slickness of their joined bodies filled the room. The heady scent of Beshel's pheromones overwhelmed Peri. He inhaled deep and let it out, repeating until it made him lightheaded. Closing his eyes, Peri let his head fall back. His mouth opened, and a groan escaped it.

Beshel sat up, wrapping his arms around Peri, bringing their bodies chest-to-chest. In this new position, Peri changed his movements. He rolled his hips up and down. His dick pressed into Beshel's furred abdomen, and Peri took advantage of the friction.

"Besh…"

Beshel sucked and gnawed at Peri's throat as he groaned and growled. Peri could feel the vibrations of the guttural sounds deep within Beshel's chest, and the direct contact with the furred skin sent them through Peri's body.

Peri moved unabashedly, fueled by an uncontrollable lust. It was imperative that he make Beshel come, and he desperately needed to come as well. Beshel pumped his own hips upward, sending his massive girth deep within Peri's ass.

"I'm going to mate you, breed you." Beshel grunted against Peri's neck, the alien's voice barely recognizable. *"Peri."*

"Yes!" Peri could feel Beshel's cock swelling inside him, pulsating, and he knew it would not be long now.

Beshel's teeth scraped against Peri's shoulder, bringing up goose bumps across Peri's skin.

"The bite is the final step."

"Yes, do it, Besh. Make me yours!"

Abruptly, Beshel stopped moving. He pulled Peri down until he was completely buried inside him, holding him in place with his muscled arms. With a roar, he clamped his teeth down onto Peri's shoulder. Beshel's cock swelled, the rings locking him inside Peri.

The scent of Degan pheromones filled the air. Peri could feel the girth of Beshel's cock throbbing, jerking powerfully, as he began pumping semen into Peri's body.

Bombarded with the multiple sensations, Peri came undone. Clinging to Beshel, he jerked against his chest, releasing his own load over and over as he cried out his mate's name.

Peri slumped against Beshel, who continued to hold him. Shudders wracked Beshel's body as the powerful orgasm continued for several more minutes.

They were forced to stay that way for some time, but Peri didn't really care. The physical closeness was like heaven after their intense lovemaking. It was the perfect way to come down from the high.

Besides, his cum was embedded in Beshel's fur, making them stuck together.

Beshel's cock was still hard, still throbbing inside him. His muscles begin to relax from their exhausting workout, and he dropped his head, loosening his grip on Beshel's back and shoulders. While resting his forehead against Beshel's shoulder, his breathing began to even and slow.

His neck and shoulder stung from the bite. Though he knew to expect it, it was still a shock to feel Besh's teeth clamp down on his skin. Speaking of the sting, his ass was stretched to the limit, and he knew he'd be sore later.

Still, Peri did not want to move. He wanted to stay like this all night.

The overpowering urge for sex had been satisfied, but Peri found he wasn't embarrassed by his behavior. It was a perfectly natural response.

"It is done," Besh whispered. "You are my bondmate, now and forever."

Epilogue

Peri looked around the yard in awe. The yard had been transformed into a wonderland for what Beshel called their bonding ceremony. He looked down at the fancy jewels on the metal sash that crossed his chest. The emeralds and diamonds that symbolized their family must have cost a fortune.

The "secret" of their mating hadn't stayed secret very long. He'd only been living with Besh for six months when the rest of the family demanded a bonding ceremony.

Truth be told, he'd put off the ceremony for as long as he could. He didn't think other people should butt their noses into their business first of all. Not to mention the thought of the ceremony scared him to death. Peri knew it didn't make any sense. It was what he had been searching for his entire life. He had Besh and together they had Hari. It was permanent. *Now and forever* Besh had said.

And they'd just said their vows in front of Beshel's entire extended family. Well, this was *his* family now as well.

He was simply amazed all of this was for him. Devin was right. Apparently the Degans didn't know how to do anything small.

He watched as Beshel cradled Hari in his arms, gently rocking the sleepy boy back and forth. Beshel looked so handsome dressed up in his vest and leather kilt. He wore a sash as well, decorated with the same jewels as Peri's.

Bastian stood next him, Dasha cradled in his arms. As they rocked to and fro, they laughed quietly with each other. The tough warriors looked like gentle giants holding onto their tiny children.

Everyone had congratulated Peri, welcoming him into the family with hugs. They fawned all over Hari, telling them how beautiful he was. Peri couldn't help but agree with them. Hari was a beautiful boy.

Devin walked up and stood at Peri's side. "You look great, *Uncle* Peri."

Peri rolled his eyes. Now that he was married to Beshel, Devin loved the fact that they were actually related; by Degan law, Peri was Devin's uncle. "Thanks. Don't tell anyone, but this skirt is pretty damn comfortable."

Devin snickered. "Told ya. It lets all your bits and pieces breathe."

Peri rolled his shoulder, trying to ease the weight of the sash. "This thing is killer though." He tugged at the hem of his tunic, trying to get it to lay flat.

"Yeah, well luckily you only need to drag that out for the really special…"

Devin's voice trailed off, and it took Peri a second to realize his friend was no longer talking.

"What?" He followed Devin's gaze down to his belly. Peri had his hand underneath his tunic, unconsciously scratching his belly button. Quickly yanking his hand free, he smoothed down the front of the shirt. "Ugh. Sorry. I know it's tacky."

"I guess that red pill doesn't work either."

"What red pill?"

"So your tummy's been itching a lot lately, huh?"

Peri narrowed his eyes. How the heck did Devin know about that? "Yeah…"

"Are you sprouting any hair there?"

Oh. *The red pill.* This line of questioning had Peri feeling sick to his itchy stomach. Again. *Oh god!* He pressed a hand against his flat belly, hoping it would help keep his breakfast down. He'd awoken with an upset stomach every morning this week. And there was no denying that he'd begun to grow quite the *happy trail* down there. He choked out the answer to Devin's question. "Yes."

Devin grinned. "Congratulations are in order, Uncle. Or should I say *Daddy*."

Peri fanned his face. *Did the temperature just jump?* "Are you saying I'm pregnant?"

He glanced around, realizing he'd said that far louder than he intended. Great. Now the entire family was staring at him. He wanted to shrink away into the ground, but before he could retreat, he was enveloped in his bondmate's arms.

Pulling him into a bear hug, Beshel lifted him off his feet. He buried his face into Peri's neck and inhaled, holding him there for a moment. "Is it true? Are you carrying another of my children?"

"It seems that way."

"You have doubly blessed me today, my love."

"Yeah?"

"Yes. Fate has blessed us with another child. For it to be so soon, it is a sign of the strength of our bond. Our family will be fruitful and successful."

"I didn't think you believed in all that."

"That was before fate led me to you, and I discovered that miracles do indeed exist."

"Corny, but I'll take it. Now shut up and kiss me."

And Besh did. Again and again.

About the Author

Rob Colton is a software developer by day, and avid reader of romance novels at night. A romantic at heart, he loves to read and write stories that feature big, burly men who find true love and happy endings.

Rob grew up in northern Michigan and currently lives in the Atlanta area with his very supportive husband and their very spoiled miniature schnauzer.

Visit Rob online:

http://robcolton.com

http://twitter.com/robcub32

http://facebook.com/robcub32

http://www.gayauthors.org/author/rob-colton

Also by Rob Colton

From Dreamspinner Press

The Ranch Foreman

An American Lamb in Europe

From Wayward Ink Publishing

The Buckle: A short in the *Stranded* Anthology

From Rob Colton

The Degan Incident (Galactic Conspiracies 1)

The Cassini Mission (Galactic Conspiracies 2)

Timber Pack Chronicles

Enforcer: Timber Pack Chronicles Book 2

Made in the USA
Coppell, TX
24 October 2021